AS

Dogs on the Case

DOGS ON THE CASE

Search Dogs Who Help Save Lives
and Enforce the Law

PATRICIA CURTIS

photographs by David Cupp

LODESTAR BOOKS · E. P. DUTTON · NEW YORK

Jacket photo of Jackpot the beagle
courtesy of Hal Fingerman

Text copyright © 1989 by Patricia Curtis
All photographs not otherwise credited are
copyright © 1989 by David Cupp
Library of Congress Cataloging-in-Publication Data

Curtis, Patricia, date
  Dogs on the case: search dogs who help save lives and enforce
the law / by Patricia Curtis; photographs by David Cupp.—1st ed.
    p.   cm.
  Bibliography: p.
  Includes index.
  Summary: Discusses dogs that are trained to use their scenting
ability to locate drugs, explosives, missing persons, agricultural
products, or other substances. Includes a directory of search-and-
rescue dog organizations.
  ISBN 0-525-67274-5
  1. Police dogs—United States—Juvenile literature. [1. Police
dogs.   2. Working dogs.]   I. Cupp, David, III.   II. Title
HV8025.C87   1989   88-37990
363.2'32–dc19   CIP
                                                      AC

Published in the United States by E. P. Dutton,
a division of Penguin Books USA Inc.

Published simultaneously in Canada by
Fitzhenry & Whiteside Limited, Toronto

Editor: Virginia Buckley

Printed in the U.S.A.   First Edition
10 9 8 7 6 5 4 3 2 1

Acknowledgments

David Cupp and I were fortunate to receive help and coop-
eration from many people in the preparation of this book.
Virtually everyone we contacted was generous with time and
attention, and we are grateful to all of them.

Several persons deserve special mention: Fran Lieser of
Search and Rescue Dogs of Colorado; Marian Hardy of
DOGS-East; Officer Steve Failla of the United States Customs
Service; Sue Rupchis, formerly of the United States Customs
Service; Officer Hal Fingerman of the United States Department of Agriculture; Officer Dutch Van Petten of the New
York City Police Canine Unit; and Trooper Doug Lancelot of
the Connecticut State Police Canine Unit. All of them read
the chapters describing their work and made helpful correc-
tions and suggestions. Thanks largely to them, the information
in this book is reliable.

In addition, David Cupp and I wish to express our appreci-
ation to Officers William Pearce, Richard Mulvaney, Edward
Wilson, and Yvonne Butler of the New York City Police
Canine Unit; Officers Charlie Rosario, Barbara Wilson, and
Herbert Herter of the United States Customs Service; search-
and-rescue team members Kim Marcom, Ann Wichmann,
and Hunter Holloway; Bonnie Aikman of the United States

· ACKNOWLEDGMENTS

Department of Agriculture; and Trooper Jim Butterworth of the Connecticut State Police Canine Unit.

We met many wonderful search dogs, but certain ones in particular earned our admiration and gratitude: Samson, Hondo, Rocky, Pockets, Boomer, Max, Gypsy, Pirate, Kiri, Jessie, Heidi, Sona, Lacy, Logan, Beto, Mojo, Buffy, Shane, Adam, Jackpot, Mattie, Rajah, and Cato.

Patricia Curtis

Contents

Dogs on the Case

The machine hasn't yet been invented that's as sensitive as a dog's nose.

—Hal Fingerman,
PPQ Canine Officer,
United States Department
of Agriculture

1
220 Million Scent Cells
About Search Dogs

One evening in the fall of 1987, a handsome golden retriever named Beto was on duty at his job at John F. Kennedy International Airport in New York. Beto worked for the United States Customs Service and was trained to use his keen nose to detect narcotics being smuggled into the United States in baggage or cargo. This night he was making a routine search of baggage coming off a plane from Central America.

The four-year-old dog worked by running along the top of the suitcases laid flat on the carousel that carried them indoors to the passengers in the baggage claim area of the airport. He was up on the carousel, jumping on one suitcase after another, detecting odors with his fine canine nose as they emanated from the baggage under his weight.

Suddenly Beto alerted to a suitcase. Instead of going on to the next, he began to bite and scratch excitedly at this particular one. His handler, Canine Enforcement Officer Charlie Rosario, ordered the suitcase set aside so the owner could be asked to open it.

The owner never showed up to claim it! Whoever he was, he must have gotten cold feet—and with good reason. When the suitcase was finally opened by the authorities, three pounds of cocaine were found inside. So, thanks to Beto,

Beto, at work at the airport, uses his nose to investigate a piece of luggage.

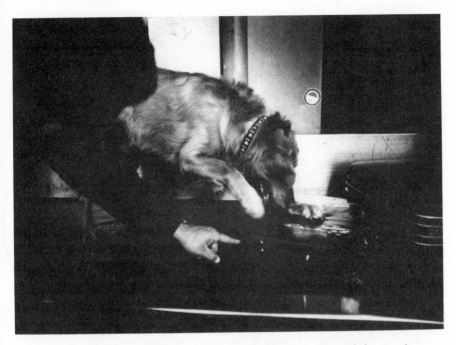

Beto has detected the scent of an illegal drug and responds by pawing and biting at the suitcase.

there were three fewer pounds of the dangerous drug sold on the streets of America, and maybe one less person taking the risk of bringing the stuff in. Beto, one of fourteen Customs Service dogs at JFK, found $60 million worth of smuggled drugs over a year's time—not bad for one dog!

Meanwhile, in the Rocky Mountains of Colorado, a two-year-old boy wandered away from his home. The sheriff called for a trained dog team from SARDOC (Search and Rescue Dogs of Colorado) and a thick-coated, black-and-white Australian shepherd named Pockets arrived with her handler, Fran Lieser. A command post for the searchers had been set up at the spot where the child was last seen. In spite of the fact that the PLS (point last seen) was heavily contaminated with human traffic and vehicle exhaust, Pockets soon picked up the little boy's trail and was on her way,

Fran Lieser starts Pockets at the PLS—the point where a missing person was last seen.

with Fran close behind her. A searching helicopter hovered overhead, following the dog below.

Suddenly the helicopter forged ahead. Thanks to Pockets, who indicated the direction in which the child had wandered, the searchers in the aircraft spotted the boy on a hilltop, landed, and gathered him up, alive and well. There's no question that Pockets would have reached the child, but the helicopter saved precious minutes. Without the dog, the airborne search party wouldn't have had any idea where to look, and a toddler's life might have been lost.

This rescue was only one of seventeen missions that members of SARDOC participated in throughout the state during the summer of 1987. There are over seventy volunteer organizations of trained search-and-rescue dog and handler teams in the United States, particularly in states with mountains and recreation areas that attract campers, hikers, climbers, skiers, and the like. They assist local law-enforcement authorities whenever the use of dogs, with their superior scenting ability, would be helpful in finding lost people. The dogs work by following the tracks of a person on the ground or the scent of a person on the vegetation along the route he or she has taken. Or the dogs may follow a person's scent that's borne on the air currents.

Teams of search-and-rescue dogs and handlers are often called upon to assist in looking for victims at disaster sites— collapsed buildings, airplane wrecks, areas hit by earthquakes, anywhere people might be trapped. A few years ago, following a terrible earthquake in Mexico City, several countries, including our own, offered assistance. Teams of dogs and handlers specially trained in disaster work volunteered to help locate people who were missing in the wreckage. Marian Hardy, a member of a Maryland-based search-and-rescue group called DOGS-East (Dogs Organized for Ground Search, East) and a national leader in this work, supervised four of the thirteen American teams that were flown to Mexico by our government. The American dog teams alone were

When a building under construction collapsed, dogs from the Connecticut State Police Canine Unit located the bodies of workers in the rubble. THE HARTFORD COURANT, A CONNECTICUT INSTITUTION SINCE 1764

successful in saving twenty-two lives. That was the first time that American dogs had been used to help following a disaster in another country. Search-and-rescue dog teams from the United States also went to El Salvador after an earthquake in 1986, and to Armenia after the devastating quake in 1988. Word is spreading about the value of search-dog teams.

State and local law-enforcement authorities also use their own canine units to help hunt for missing people—lost children, wandering mental patients, people trapped in wreckage—or to track down escaped prisoners or criminals on the run. Often dogs are asked to find evidence necessary for the prosecution of a crime—the handgun a mugger threw away, for example, or the wallet a thief tossed in the bushes to avoid having it found on him should he be stopped and searched.

Dogs are trained to find bombs and other explosive devices. The United States Department of Agriculture uses dogs to detect illegal plants and food being brought in from other countries. Some exterminating companies even use dogs to locate termites. The federal Environmental Protection Agency is experimenting with training dogs to find hazardous wastes, gas pipe leaks, and underground gasoline tanks. Some states use dogs to catch hunters trying to smuggle game, pelts, or songbirds they have killed illegally.

"The use of dogs is limited only by human imagination," says Trooper Doug Lancelot of the Connecticut State Police Canine Unit.

What is it that all these dogs have in common? They are all trained to use their amazing scenting ability to locate substances, whether human skin or clothing, explosives, drugs, agricultural products, food, or anything else their owners or handlers need them to find. Though the Department of Agriculture uses beagles, most of the dogs who do this work are medium-sized or large: dogs such as shepherds, retrievers, rottweilers, Doberman pinschers, and bloodhounds, or mixed breeds with this type of ancestry. But whatever their size or breed, they all have good noses.

The Dog's Amazing Nose

We all know that dogs have superior hearing and can detect sounds that are inaudible to us. But if we think their hearing ability is pretty great, in truth it's not nearly as impressive as their remarkable talent for scent detection. Everyone who has a pet dog knows that dogs seem to be continually sniffing—the ground, trees, air, objects, people, other dogs. But it's not just curiosity or habit that makes them do it; this is how they obtain and process most of their information about the world.

As a species, dogs are equipped with noses that are remarkably well built for scenting. The nasal passages are designed to receive and trap odors; the scent nerves are comparatively large and numerous. The scenting ability of human beings is not highly developed; we have an estimated 5 million olfactory cells—that is, cells used for smelling—concentrated in a relatively small area at the back of the nose. By comparison, dogs' noses have scent cells spread over a large area; small dogs have an estimated 125 million, medium-sized dogs about 145 million, and big dogs such as German shepherds are thought to have as many as 220 million scent cells!

Long-nosed breeds with wide nostrils are naturally more efficient smellers than short-nosed dogs. Some toy breeds have such little noses that their nasal blood vessels, nerves, bones, and tissues are abnormally cramped, and their nostrils are small or deformed. But even so, their noses are several hundred times more sensitive than ours. Any dog can detect odors that are totally imperceptible to a human being.

Not only do dogs have a marvelous ability to detect scents—they are good at distinguishing one odor from another and remembering it. The part of a dog's brain that receives messages from the nerves of the nose is highly developed and can store up scent information like a computer. You might notice that sometimes a dog will fail to recognize at a distance people or other dogs that he knows, until he gets within range to identify their scent.

In addition to this scenting ability, dogs are intelligent animals. And what's just as important, from our point of view, is that they are almost infinitely trainable. They have lived in close association with human beings since prehistoric times, and they are by nature social animals. In the wild, all canine species—wolves, coyotes, and the like—live in packs with clearly defined behavior among themselves. They observe rituals, display greeting behavior, and are sensitive to one another's emotional states. Each pack has a leader—an adult who, by virtue of strength and dominant personality, is regarded by the others as the alpha, or top dog. The other

One characteristic all search dogs have in common is a good nose. TOP RIGHT: *A.J. KMIECIK/THE PRESS-ENTERPRISE*

pack members defer to him and look to him for direction and protection, and for maintaining order. (Because female dogs are often preoccupied with pregnancy and caring for pups, the pack leader among wild canine species is typically male.)

The natural habitat of all domestic dogs, whatever their breed, is the human home. Living with us, as our companions or helpers, under our protection and care, they regard us as their pack leaders. That's why they can be trained, whether it is for work such as rounding up sheep or for play such as fetching a ball or rolling over on command. In the eyes of a pet or helpmate dog, his owner, man, woman, or child—whoever feeds him, walks him, and cares for him—is pack leader. Instinctively, he can be trained to do whatever the leader commands.

Nobody knows how long and in how many ways human beings have made use of the dog's extraordinary scenting ability. Dogs have been finding lost livestock and tracking down game for their masters probably as long as dogs and humans have lived together.

People have sometimes come to take their dogs' ability for granted. "I live in an isolated area in the mountains," says a man in Vermont. "I take my dog hiking with me, and I never worry about getting lost, because I've taught him to retrace our steps by tracking. When I'm ready to turn back, I say to him, 'Let's go home.' He knows that's the command for him to follow the scent of our tracks and lead us home the way we came."

But in spite of the fact that the scenting ability of dogs is well known, in modern times it has become more usual to rely on technology for many of the services that dogs formerly performed. As ingenious machines and devices were invented and refined, the use of dogs declined. It was assumed that a machine is always better at a task than an animal. Trooper Doug Lancelot suggests that perhaps our American faith in machines made authorities reluctant, in the past, to use dogs for important detection work, despite the fact that using dogs could save massive amounts of manpower, money, and time.

However, that is changing. There seems to be a new recognition that dogs are often better at many jobs than machines are. "In some situations, dogs can make the use of machines obsolete," states Doug.

That is why the training of dogs for many kinds of scent detection work is increasing.

Teamwork

It is important to bear in mind that training a dog for any of the jobs based on scent detection is not forcing the animal to do something that is unnatural. It is building on a talent that the animal has anyway, and channeling it in a way that does not harm him. Scent detection work does not distort a dog's natural ability, nor does it exploit him. In almost all instances, this use of dogs is for the good of people, without commercial profit.

In addition, scent detection work, with responsible people, does not violate the historic bond that exists between human beings and domestic dogs. Most dogs enter the world ready to be friendly, and when they are not, something has usually gone very wrong. Dogs that attack people indiscriminately and cause serious harm have most likely been brutalized by violent training and cruel treatment or by lack of human companionship as puppies. They hate and fear people, often including their owners, and with good reason, considering how they are treated. They are an example of how the normal bond between human beings and dogs has been twisted and broken, or never developed.

The relationship between scent detector dogs and their owners or handlers is one of profound trust, respect, and love. Whether the animal is a trained search-and-rescue dog, a bomb detector dog, a police patrol dog, or any other dog doing scent detection work, the animal is ready to do what his teammate asks—to put his life on the line, if necessary, for him or her.

Punishment is never used in the training of scent detector dogs. They aren't trained to perform in order to avoid pain. They may be corrected, sometimes scolded, and are often made to repeat an exercise until they get it right, but they are never struck or "put in the doghouse" for making mistakes.

They work for reward. The reward is always praise and

A search-and-rescue dog jumps up for a hug from her owner.

petting, sometimes with a treat, too, or a few minutes of play with their owner. In any kind of training, even when a pet dog is taught to do tricks, what the animal values most is "Good dog!" and a pat or a big hug. Search dogs work because they are made to feel important, they know they have a job, they want to please their handlers, and they are rewarded when they find what they're looking for.

The person who is the other member of a search team is as highly trained as the dog. Members of police canine units, for example, must first be police officers with superior records. To be a canine enforcement officer in the Customs Service, you must have already worked in a division of the service, or have had canine experience in military service. You are interviewed closely before you enter training, and supervised throughout. To be a member of a volunteer search-and-rescue canine outfit, you must spend years of training with your dog, learn many search-and-rescue skills, and be certified by an official governing group.

Being the handler of a dog in scent detection work is active and demanding. It is often exciting, always challenging, sometimes dangerous. Above all, it is frequently rewarding when you and your dog find what you are looking for.

2
"I'm Going to Turn Him Loose!"
Police Patrol Dogs

"This is the police!" shouted Police Officer Richard Mulvaney as he stood just inside the door of the building, holding Samson by the collar. "I have a trained dog. If you don't come out, I'm going to turn him loose!"

It was only a training exercise, but to Samson it might as well have been the real thing, with a criminal suspect hiding in the abandoned building. The handsome German shepherd was very alert and excited. He knew his job. When the officer released his leash, telling Samson to "Go find him!" the dog charged down the hall, trying to pick up a scent.

"A suspect often comes out as soon as he hears I've got a dog," said Richard. "But sometimes he thinks the dog won't find him. Also, there may be more than one person in hiding. I direct Samson to search the whole building, even after he finds someone and starts to bark. When I'm occupied putting handcuffs on one suspect, I don't want somebody else shooting me in the back."

Samson dashed back and forth through the halls until Richard ordered him upstairs alone while he remained in a protected position in the front entryway. Samson could be heard thundering around throughout the vacant three-story building. Soon he began to bark furiously.

Officer Richard Mulvaney gets Samson ready to search the abandoned building in which a "suspect" is hiding.

In this building search exercise, Police Officer "Dutch" Van Petten was playing the role of the suspect. He had hoisted himself up on a shelf in a closet. Had he been an armed and dangerous criminal, he could have gotten a good shot at anyone who was looking for him. Samson found him soon enough and stood barking aggressively up at him. Satisfied that Samson would also have found and barked at anyone else hiding in the building, Richard now called the dog off and put him in the sit/stay position. "Good boy!" the officer said warmly. Samson accepted the praise gravely, but as he sat, he was businesslike, still on the alert.

As Richard pretended to put handcuffs on Dutch, the "suspect" made a break and ran down the hall. "Get him!" yelled Richard. Samson made a running hit, grabbing Dutch by the forearm and holding on as he had been trained. Dutch was wearing a padded sleeve for protection; otherwise his arm might have been painfully bruised.

If Dutch had not tried to run, causing Richard to give Samson the order to get him, the dog would only have threatened and barked. In an earlier training exercise, with Police Officer Yvonne Butler playing the role of the suspect, a dog named Hondo kept her standing stock still until his handler, Police Officer Edward Wilson, arrived a few seconds later. Hondo did not leap for Yvonne's arm until she made a motion to run and his handler ordered him to grab her.

The value of the dog in a building search is great, and police departments in cities all over the United States have canine units for this purpose, among others. Without a dog, many officers would have to spread out, putting themselves in danger, and take perhaps hours to comb every corner of a building. A well-hidden suspect might elude detection because the officers, being human, have only their eyes and ears to help them, while a dog has the added advantage of those extra millions of scent cells in his nose.

Officer Dutch Van Petten is the trainer in the canine program of the New York City Police Department. Officer Richard

"Here he is! I've found him!" Samson seems to be saying.

Mulvaney is the assistant trainer, and Samson is his dog. Officers Wilson and Butler were members of a class in training to become canine officers, with their dogs, Hondo and Rocky. The canine program is based on the grounds of an unused army post; one of the empty buildings is ideal for building search exercises.

The Canine Unit Team

Police officers—men and women—are not assigned to become canine officers; they apply for the privilege. They must have already finished their two-year probation period on the police force with a good record. They must pass an interview to assess their general understanding of police work and their good judgment. In addition, they are given a psychological examination to assure, among other factors, that they have the right attitude to be in charge of a dog. Then, if they are accepted, they enter a class of five or six officers and dogs under the direction of Officer Dutch Van Petten.

The training of an officer-and-dog team takes fourteen weeks, including one week of night work. During this time, the officers are continually judged on their ability to follow orders, to learn, to think clearly in sudden, unexpected situations, and on the way they interact with their dogs. "I want to be sure the officers and dogs are well matched to each other," says Dutch. The bond between dog and handler must be tight.

"A regular police officer has a gun as a weapon, but a canine officer has not only a gun but a tool—a dog—that can become another weapon," Dutch explains. "The officer must be doubly able to make good decisions in all kinds of situations."

Previous professional experience with dogs is not required of the officers entering canine work. However, dogs of the New York City Police Department do not live in kennels or at police stations—they live at home with their handlers. There's a very good reason for this: The dogs must be well socialized, not hostile or afraid of people. These are not attack dogs. Every dog must be capable of catching and holding a person on command, and of defending his handler and himself, but he must have a good temperament and be safe to work among crowds of people. Some of the dogs are reserved with strangers, and do not respond to petting with wagging tails and kisses, but neither do they bite or snap.

Officer Dutch Van Petten's dog, Boomer, lives at home with the officer, his wife, and two young daughters. Samson lives with Officer Richard Mulvaney and his wife. Rocky lives with Officer Yvonne Butler and her ten-year-old daughter, Sharifa. "Rocky loves children," says Yvonne.

All the dogs of the New York City Police are unneutered male German shepherds. "Most municipal police worldwide use German shepherds," says Dutch. "These dogs are thought to be intelligent, capable of aggression, and to have an exceptionally good sense of smell."

As every dog owner knows, male dogs, especially those that are unneutered, are frequently quarrelsome with others of the same sex. Nevertheless, the German shepherds of the canine unit learn to get along with one another.

The dogs must be one or two years old and in perfect health when they enter this work. Some continue until they are seven or eight. These animals are large—one dog weighs in at 105 pounds! Many are given to the police by their owners, others are bought with funds donated by the public.

Sometimes an officer flunks or drops out of training, and sometimes a dog reaches a learning plateau and can't progress beyond it in the time the training course requires. Or the rigorous training may ask more of a dog than he can do physically. The dogs develop stamina and agility on an obstacle course in a training field at the canine center. They must be able to leap over a six-foot wall, a ten-foot horizontal barrier, and through an open window. They must climb a ladder, and they must obey when taught to sit or lie atop a structure. Their response to obedience commands, of course, must be absolute. They learn both voice and hand signals.

Dogs that don't make it are usually kept by their handlers—the officers don't want to give them up, so they become family pets. Or the dogs may be given to other police officers as pets. As a last resort, they may be surrendered to the ASPCA, where they are put up for adoption.

At the end of the fourteen weeks, the officer trainees must pass a written exam, and if they have satisfied all other aspects of their training, they are certified as fit for duty as canine officers. After being assigned to precincts, they patrol their assigned neighborhoods alone with their dogs. They also take part in any raid where a trained search dog would be needed.

But that's not the end of it. Every canine officer must exercise his or her dog in obedience daily, and come to the training center once a month to keep up certification. The dogs must maintain their skills and never forget what they have learned.

Search Training

After the building search, Samson was asked to perform another type of search, a box search. Out on the training field, six or eight large boxes the size of sheds, big enough for a man to hide in, were spaced several yards apart. Without being seen, Officer Dutch Van Petten, again playing the role of a crime suspect, hid in one of them.

Officer Richard Mulvaney approached with Samson on the leash and repeated the warning: "This is the police! I have a trained dog. If you don't come out, I'm going to turn him loose!"

After a moment, he released Samson's leash. Streaking across the field, Samson lost no time in alerting to the box that was Dutch's hiding place. His handler directed him to check every box. Samson obeyed, but quickly raced back to Dutch's box. Richard put the dog in a sit position beside him and ordered the "criminal" to come out. Dutch shuffled out. "I ain't done nothin'," he said, playing his part.

But then he pulled his gun. "Freeze!" yelled Richard. As Dutch fired a blank and began to run, Samson was on him, forcing him to drop the gun. No dog in the police force can afford to be gun-shy.

Now Richard ordered the dog to a sit/stay position some fifteen to twenty feet away while he pretended to frisk and handcuff the "perpetrator." Samson, as alert as a dog can be, never took his eyes off the suspect. Suddenly, Dutch slightly shifted his position in a threatening manner. As if he were shot out of a cannon, Samson cleared the distance between them almost in one leap and again grabbed Dutch's arm.

"He interpreted Dutch's movement as an aggressive act against me. To Samson, freeze means freeze," explained Richard. He then gave Samson the command "Out!" which told the dog to let go.

Dutch thinks that dogs in training may regard these search exercises as games, though they behave seriously. Certainly Samson showed no hostility whatever toward Dutch when the exercises were over. "But when a dog is out on the street with his handler, he recognizes tension and danger. He knows when he or his handler is threatened," says the officer.

Police dogs will attack under three conditions: when ordered by their handlers, when they perceive that their handlers are threatened, or when they themselves are threatened.

The police explain that this superprotective behavior can be triggered only by the animal's handler. The dog acquires this through what is called the "agitate" part of the training, when he learns to obey the command "Get him!" only when it comes from his handler. If anyone else orders the dog to attack, the dog won't pay any attention.

However, a dog is trained to obey other commands from

A box search exercise: Samson detects the "suspect," who comes out of the hiding place when ordered to by the officer.

When the "suspect" tries to flee, Samson is on him at once.

other officers—for instance, if a canine officer is shot down and others are trying to rescue him, his dog must allow someone else to approach and move him.

After Police Officer Yvonne Butler finished her training and was assigned to a precinct with Rocky, a situation arose in which Rocky demonstrated his awareness and protective behavior. Yvonne and Rocky were on patrol on a busy city street when a photographer aimed his camera at them. Rocky noticed instantly and objected. To the dog, the camera looked like a weapon. Yvonne, who weighs 110 pounds, successfully kept Rocky, who weighs 85, under control; otherwise the photographer might have had to answer to Rocky for following the dog and handler and pointing a threatening device at them.

Tracking

The building and box searches, with the dog off the lead and ordered to grab and hold a suspect, are called aggressive searches. Police dogs also perform what's called a friendly search, usually on the leash and tracking—that is, following the scent of a person along the ground. This is used when the dog and his handler are asked to search for a missing person—a lost child, for example. Sometimes Dutch's dog, Boomer, practices this kind of search with one of the Van Petten daughters. Behind Boomer's back, the little girl will hide somewhere in the neighborhood, and Boomer will track her down.

Occasionally a police dog is called upon to use his tracking ability to find a criminal. Dutch tells of a dog that was taken to the scene of a homicide. A man had been assaulted in his apartment, then had staggered to the lobby of the building and died. The dog was taken to the man's apartment, picked up the scent of the killer, and, undistracted by the hundreds of other human scents along the way, tracked the criminal for half a mile over concrete, asphalt, and grass, till he found him hiding under a bridge.

Officer Yvonne Butler patrols a tough neighborhood with Rocky, her trained dog.

When a dog is tracking or trailing, he follows the scent of a particular human being on the ground or vegetation. However, a good dog will also follow air scent, as do dogs on search-and-rescue missions. Every human body gives off what's called a scent cone—the person is in the center or tip of an invisible cone, and his or her scent emanates outward and around in a cone shape, strongest near the person and growing fainter as the cone enlarges. A dog air-scenting may move his head from side to side, or zigzag back and forth, trying to keep the scent in focus as he runs.

"One of our canine officers was on a routine patrol in a park when his dog alerted and led him off the path into a clump of bushes some distance away," Dutch relates. "The officer found a mugging victim, unconscious. After he radioed for help and got the guy taken to a hospital, he had the dog search the area. The dog found the man's wallet, eyeglasses, and other personal things."

Police dogs often make article searches, looking for items around the scene of a crime that can be used as evidence in court. The dog may work on or off the leash. In these cases, the dog doesn't know exactly what he's looking for, so if he is working off lead, he'll just bring whatever he finds to his handler and continue until he hits on the evidence—a knife, wallet, gun, or tool such as a screwdriver that might have been used in the commission of a crime.

Samson performed an article search as a training exercise. An officer planted his gun under a car, well concealed inside the rear bumper. Samson didn't know exactly what he was looking for, but he knew he was supposed to locate some object with fresh human scent on it. The car with the gun was parked among several other cars.

"Attaboy!" called Richard as Samson circled each car, sniffing. "Keep looking." Officers continually talk to their dogs to keep up their motivation during a search.

Within a few minutes, Samson located the place where the gun was hidden, but couldn't get it out immediately. He

An article search exercise: A gun has been planted inside the bumper of a car; Samson finds it and carefully removes it.

Samson carries the gun to his handler.

pawed at the bumper carefully, finally extracted the gun with his teeth, and carried it in his mouth to his handler.

These brave and well-trained dogs are a credit to the New York City police force and to their skillful and patient handlers. The dogs' superior ability at scent detection is used to help protect the city's citizens.

3
Someone's Life Is on the Line

Wilderness Search-and-Rescue Dogs

Fran Lieser sat under a tree in the quiet of the hot summer afternoon, wondering if Max would be able to find her. Early that morning, she had taken a different route to this same spot, about two miles from her house, but her scent on that trail would now be nearly six hours old. Max was an experienced search-and-rescue dog, but this practice operation was being carried out in ninety-five-degree heat, and the scent might have drifted or been trapped in the thickly wooded ravine below her. Also, Fran had seen two does with fawns nearby. Would Max be distracted by them?

Fran, a tanned and curly-haired woman in her late thirties, is the Colorado search dog coordinator and a unit instructor of SARDOC (Search and Rescue Dogs of Colorado). SARDOC teams consisting of handlers and their dogs are important adjuncts to accredited search-and-rescue organizations. All are volunteers. Like other search-and-rescue dog teams, they assist local authorities when a person is reported missing: a lost child, elderly person, mental patient, hiker or camper, disaster victim, or suspected crime victim. When the sheriff of Fran's county wants dogs to assist in a search mission, he calls her. It is up to her to respond with one of her trained dogs, and to call out as many other handlers and their dogs as may be needed.

From her home in the gently rolling countryside of the eastern foothills of the Rocky Mountains, Fran also conducts regular training and practice exercises with the members of her SARDOC unit. Max, a Doberman pinscher, and his owner, Chris McKelvey, like all members of dog-and-handler teams, have to practice every week to keep up their skills.

Fran listened but could hear no one coming. If Max was on the ball, she thought, he and Chris should be here by now. The shimmering heat slightly blurred the sight of the near-distant mountains. Suddenly she could discern the sound of movement in the brush. Within seconds the Doberman bounded up the slope to her with his tall, blonde owner scrambling through the bushes behind him.

"He picked up your scent on the air a little ways back, so I let him off the lead," said Chris. Fran and Chris spent a few minutes rewarding Max with praise and petting.

Search-and-rescue dogs are taught to trail or to air-scent, or both. When trailing, the dog follows the scent a person has left on the ground or vegetation. If weather conditions and terrain are ideal, a good trailing dog can follow a trail that's as much as forty-eight hours old, though in extreme heat, twelve hours would be about the maximum. When working, the dog may trail as much as fifty feet from the actual route the person took if the scent has drifted.

Heat is especially hard on a search dog, because it is difficult for the animal to pant and sniff at the same time. Also, temperature at ground level may be as much as twenty degrees hotter than at six feet above the ground.

But a good trailing dog will also use air scent—the scent carried on the air currents from the cone-shaped aura of scent given off by a human body. And some dogs are air-scent dogs only. "Many dogs simply cannot or will not trail," says Fran. "Yet, if wind and terrain are right, they can pick up the scent of a human body, alive or dead, as much as a

On an actual search mission: A handler holds a ribbon to determine wind direction. Her dog, standing downwind, can tell in seconds if the victim is in the rocky ravine.

mile away. It's a beautiful sight to see a dog air-scenting, running head up, full of confidence, ears alert, eyes and nose going. Sometimes on a mission we use a trailing dog to show us the general direction a victim has taken, and then we fan out with air-scent dogs."

Air-scenting dogs are very important in mountainous country. Let's say a hiker takes a long, winding route up a peak and then falls and hurts himself. He's reported missing, and a search team including several dogs and handlers is assembled to look for him. A trailing dog sets out from the PLS (point last seen), and the others spread out over the area, zigzagging, trying to pick up the scent cone. One dog gets within a mile of the hiker and suddenly catches his scent on the air. Instead of following the wandering path the hiker took, the dog leads her handler directly up the peak to him, saving several miles and perhaps several hours.

"When a dog alerts to air scent, we follow her as fast as we can," explains Fran. "If the dog is quite far ahead of us when she finds the victim, we know she'll race back and lead us to him. When someone's life is on the line, minutes count."

The Search-and-Rescue Dog Team

When you mention the words "search-and-rescue dog," many people think of a Saint Bernard with a little flask of brandy attached to his collar. It's a popular image, but such a dog does not exist, at least not in any modern search-and-rescue team in any country. He was probably invented by a brandy company to advertise its product.

However, it is true that in the eighteenth and nineteenth centuries, Saint Bernards lived at a hospice, or refuge for travelers, run by monks in the Swiss Alps. Legend has it that those dogs heroically found many helpless persons lost in snowstorms in the rugged and treacherous mountain passes. However, those huge dogs are not trained for search-and-rescue work today, having been replaced, worldwide, by smaller, more nimble breeds.

And many people think all search dogs are bloodhounds. In movies, fugitives are sometimes pursued by packs of slavering, ferocious-looking bloodhounds. Actually, these dogs normally love people. The joke among bloodhound owners is: "When they catch someone, the danger is they'll lick him to death!" These hefty, brawny dogs are good trackers, working with their noses to the ground, and are members of search-and-rescue outfits in many parts of the United States. However, bloodhounds are not generally used in rugged mountainous terrain or at disaster sites where the victims' trails don't exist.

The idea of training dogs for wilderness search originated in the United States, based on the dogs used in the mountains of France, Germany, and Switzerland to search for victims of avalanches. Today, European dog-and-handler teams are less experienced in wilderness search than those in this country are.

SARDOC dogs, unlike the New York City Police Department canines, are a mixed group. They can be most any medium-to-large breed or mixed breed weighing between about 45 and 100 pounds. In addition to Max the Doberman, SARDOC dogs include Australian shepherds, German shepherds, Labrador retrievers, Chesapeake Bay retrievers, golden retrievers, bloodhounds, a Border collie, and a medium-sized terrier mix.

Females outnumber males. All are neutered. All are friendly and outgoing. "A good search-and-rescue dog must have a high opinion of people," Fran points out. "In order to work long and hard—in often difficult situations—to find someone, the dogs must really think people are worth finding; otherwise, they might figure, why bother? Their training must preserve their high regard for and trust of people. Some of our dogs will do anything to find people."

Search-and-rescue dogs are owned by their handlers and live in their homes. They are chosen by their owners more or less the way we acquire our companion dogs: purchased, found, adopted, perhaps received as gifts.

"I met my dog, Logan, at a party!" states Ann Wichmann, a ranger for the Boulder Mountain Parks system. "Someone brought a litter of ten-week-old black Labrador pups to find homes for. I fell in love with him on the spot. His entire behavior was so scent oriented, I was sure he'd make a great search dog, and he is."

Today, four-year-old Logan is certified for air scent, avalanche, and water search. "He's even good at finding evidence and objects people have lost," says Ann proudly. "Recently, a visitor to the park lost her handbag. Logan worked over the wide area where she thought she might have dropped it, and kept bringing me things. After a few minutes he came trotting up to me with her purse in his mouth."

When dogs on search missions, real or practice, find the victims, they are rewarded with extravagant petting and praise, hugs and kisses, maybe even a few minutes of play. Handlers in training are taught that the first thing they must do when their dogs lead them to victims, on actual missions or in training, is reward their dogs—even before tending to the victims. "First, reward the dog!" is the rule. This may sound like a callous disregard for the victims, who may be suffering from broken bones or exposure, but actually, on real missions, the handlers are accompanied by other searchers, who take care of the victims immediately. The point is that the dogs, who have found the persons in the first place, perhaps saving lives, must be made to feel they have done a good job and won approval. Experienced dogs may even reward themselves by finding a stick to play with; they know they have done their job and are proud of it.

As for the brandy that the Saint Bernards are believed to have carried in little flasks on their collars for the victims they found in the snow, and the whiskey that is offered to all kinds of accident victims in the movies—that just doesn't happen in real search-and-rescue operations. According to Hunter Holloway, an active Colorado mountain rescue leader, you must first warm the body core of a victim who is suffering from hypothermia, or severe cold from exposure. This is done by giving the victim warm, moist oxygen—never brandy, not even warm soup. If a victim needs oxygen, it is quickly brought from the base camp of the mission.

Unless she is working in very thick underbrush where a harness might get caught, a SARDOC dog on a rescue mission wears a red harness with a sleigh bell on it. This is not for decoration or to make the dog look cute. First of all, putting the harness on tells the dog she's going to work. During a night search, a light can be attached to the harness. The harness helps protect the dog during hunting season: Just as hunters wear orange to keep themselves from being mistakenly shot by fellow hunters, it is hoped that the color of the harness and the sound of the bell signal a hunter that the dog is not a wild animal crashing in the underbrush. A hunter once told Fran that if her dog hadn't been wearing the identifying red harness, he would have shot the dog on sight. A dog might scare away the deer, he said, spoiling his chance to kill them.

But the main reason for the harness and bell is to reassure the victim. Some people, especially when they're lost and scared to begin with, might panic on seeing a rather large dog bounding toward them. In rugged country, if they tried to run from the dog, they could hurt or even kill themselves. But almost everyone seeing a dog wearing a red harness and a merry bell would perceive the animal as harmless. Children make up a significant proportion of lost persons; the bright harness and jingle bell can reduce any fear they might feel.

Also, a person who has been lost for several days and is badly frightened might imagine he is being attacked by a dog running up to him, and defend himself accordingly. In one instance, a missing fifteen-year-old hunter was found by a big friendly search-and-rescue dog who wasn't wearing a collar or harness. The dog, in his joy at finding the boy, put his paws on the boy's shoulders in order to lick his face. But the boy lost his head. Apparently unable to tell the difference between a dog and a wild animal, he imagined he was being attacked. In what might be regarded as a typical hunter reaction, he gutted the dog with his hunting knife, killing the valuable and highly trained animal who had saved his life.

Search-and-rescue dogs have their own style of trailing and of greeting a victim. "My Australian shepherd dog Pockets usually works just a few feet ahead of me, though on a fresh trail she can be long gone, out of sight," says Fran. "She runs back every now and then to be sure I'm coming—I'll see her pop back over a hill to check on me. I just keep heading for the last place I saw her, and sooner or later, she'll show up again to lead me."

The dogs also have their own way of responding to a victim, depending partly on what the victim is doing when they get there. Some dogs stand and bark. "Come here, I found him!" they seem to say. "Game's over and I won." Other dogs wag their tails and try to lick the victim's face.

The SARDOC handlers range in age from eighteen to fifty-five, and come from many occupations. Fran works weekdays as a computer software supervisor; Chris works as a ski patroller on Aspen Mountain. Another handler, Barbara May, is an elementary school teacher; Kim Marcom is a graduate student at a nearby college. Among the others are a police dispatcher and a college professor. "We had a junior high schooler in training with us who was terrific, and so was her dog," says Fran. "But she had to drop out—it interfered with her schoolwork. We hope she'll come back after she's finished her schooling."

While search-and-rescue teams are made up mostly of men, search-and-rescue dog handlers, nationwide, are more often women. To be accepted as a member of SARDOC, a person must be physically strong, very patient, and highly committed. Training can take three years of hard, consistent work, several times a week, in all weather. Practice must continue weekly, year round, permanently.

"The drop-out rate is fairly high," comments Fran. "Some people think they can spend a day or two in training with their dogs and go right out on a mission. They're not prepared for the hundreds of hours of training exercises.

"Also, besides training with their dogs, they must learn map reading and compass navigation, radio communication, . basic survival skills. They have to know how to dress for a mission and what kind of gear to carry. On a mission, SARDOC handlers might have to carry food and water for themselves and their dogs for forty-eight hours, so they must know what kind of food to carry for both, and when and how much to eat and drink.

On a search-and-rescue mission a dog handler must carry water for herself and her dog.

"Search-and-rescue work is greatly needed, exciting, and highly rewarding. But it is also a serious and sometimes dangerous activity, not a casual hobby."

When a mission is called for in high country, it is not unusual for a SARDOC team to be airlifted to the search area. Both dog and handler must be perfectly at home in a helicopter. To protect their sensitive ears, the dogs wear earplugs or earmuffs, held in place with bandanas.

Fran ties earmuffs on Pockets and leads her onto the helicopter.

SARDOC teams are certified, when ready, by the standards committee, which is elected by the members. All who go on actual search missions must be certified.

Training a SARDOC Dog

There is some latitude in the age range within which a dog can join a SARDOC training group; he or she can be a pup or a few years old. Kiri, for example, was a gangling German shepherd puppy; Max the Doberman had been obedience-trained but was already three years old when he entered search-dog training. However, no dog under two years of age is used on a real search mission. Some can continue to work until they're ten or twelve.

After Max found Fran in that afternoon practice session, the two women and the dog returned to Fran's property, where other members of the SARDOC unit were resting under the trees, waiting to complete some exercises in trailing and air scenting.

In a trailing exercise, one person walks away a half-mile or more from Fran's property, setting little red flags on stakes in the ground to mark his or her trail, and then hiding. A dog and handler then set out to find the "victim." The dog—who operates much more by scent than by visual clues—ignores the flags, but the flags help the handler know if the dog is on the right trail or losing the scent.

This day, several inexperienced dogs and handlers were training with experienced teams who were practicing. In the case of young dogs just learning to trail, the owners often play the part of the victim, for the dogs are naturally eager to find their owners. Kiri had found hers with only a little help.

It was Jessie's turn. "Scott is playing the victim," said Terry, the golden retriever's owner. "He has laid a trail in that direction and is hiding in the grass somewhere." Terry pointed to some distant fields of tall yellow grass.

Terry had a worn shirt of Scott's in a plastic bag, which

A young dog in training follows a "victim's" trail, finds her, and is rewarded with praise and petting.

she removed carefully and held for Jessie to smell. A scent object must be something the victim has worn or handled recently that hasn't been handled by others. Search teams keep a scent object in a clean plastic bag so it won't confuse the dog by having the scent of others on it. And they're careful not to use plastic garbage bags that may contain deodorant.

With Jessie on a long lead, Terry set off across the road and into the field, following the red flags that Scott had placed several yards apart. Because of the heat, Jessie left the flagged trail several times to follow Scott's scent, which had drifted in the slight breeze, but she continued in the right general direction. At one point, she lost the scent in a ditch and had to trot back and forth several times before she picked it up again, climbed out of the ditch, and kept going.

Jessie soon discovered Scott lying on the ground and, wagging her tail, licked Scott's face with great enthusiasm. "Good dog, good dog!" exclaimed Terry, hugging Jessie.

There are of course situations in which trailing is not useful or possible. When the trail of a missing person is too old, when there is no scent object to help a dog know whom she is looking for, and especially at disaster scenes where there may be multiple victims—in such instances, skilled air-scenting dogs are needed. At the scene of an earthquake, a mud slide, or an airplane wreck—where bodies may be scattered for miles—dogs move in zigzag patterns seeking scent cones, and then work toward the centers of the cones. In good terrain and weather conditions, they can detect a human scent at a distance of even a mile.

Once a dog has learned basic trailing, air-scent lessons can begin. A team member, instead of laying a trail and hiding at the end of it, loops back upwind so his or her scent will be carried downwind toward the dog, and hides at a point about halfway. The dog in the process of trailing picks up the scent on the air, and is then encouraged to forget about following the trail and head directly to the "victim." If an air-scenting dog on an actual search mission is upwind from the victim, she may even pass the area where the victim is until she gets downwind and can pick up his scent; then she circles back and finds him.

Training the dog is only part of the teamwork. "You have to learn to interpret every movement your dog makes—what it means when her tail is up or down, ears up or down, and the like—because she is telling you something and it's up to you to read it correctly," Fran says.

Another part of the training of a SARDOC dog takes place at the obstacle course. Situated on Fran's property, a collection of ladders, tires, planks, and oil drums is set up to imitate or approximate conditions a dog might encounter at a disaster site. After the trailing and air-scenting exercises this hot afternoon, the SARDOC members gave their dogs some training exercises on the obstacles.

A ladder led to a high platform that was somewhat unsteady. Normally, a dog would be afraid to walk across anything unstable, much less go up and down a ladder. But if a trained dog is to search a collapsed building or any other accident scene where victims might be trapped, she must be confident enough to climb and walk on shaky structures. One at a time, the dogs—Gypsy, Max, Pirate, Jessie—went up the ladder, then down it head first. Some needed a lot of boosting from their owners and encouragement from Fran, who was perched on top of the platform.

While some dogs tried the ladders, others worked at a series of large tires fastened together and suspended several feet above the ground. At the command "Through!" each dog jumped up and crawled through the tires, which swayed slightly under her weight. This took some coaxing and usually a boost from the dog's handler, but she was cheered onward and praised lavishly when she emerged at the other end.

On the SARDOC obstacle course: An experienced dog climbs the ladder while another wonders if she should try it.

Gypsy is doing her best, but needs a boost.

At the other end of the high platform, a dog heading down the ladder will be helped until she gets the hang of it.

Gypsy emerges triumphantly from the hanging tires.

The dogs crawled through cylinders of different diameters and under tent-like structures so they would learn to be comfortable even in tight places. When they balanced on the rounded sides of oil drums, they got the hang of pulling in their toenails and standing flat on their footpads so they wouldn't slide off.

If the work on the obstacle course looked at times like dogs training to do tricks in a circus, and seemed like a game to the dogs, it was all serious training. Someday, at any time, a person trapped in wreckage could be located and saved by a dog fearless and experienced enough to search in conditions much like those of the obstacle course.

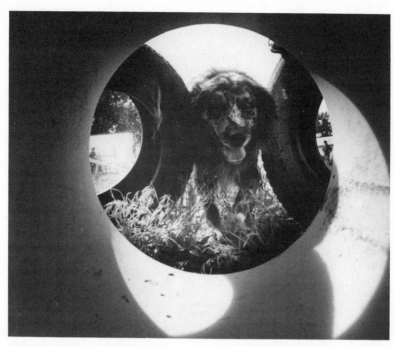

Every search-and-rescue dog must learn to go fearlessly through tight places, jump over obstacles, and walk on unsteady or slanting planks.

Below: *Park ranger Ann Wichmann trains her dog, Logan, in a playground, teaching him to pull in his toenails and stand flat on his footpads so he won't slip on rounded or slanting surfaces.*

Missions

"When someone is lost, the sheriff is the first person notified, and he sets the mission in motion," explains Fran. "He'll call me, and I'll try to get all the information I can: How long has the victim been missing? What are the weather conditions at the moment, and what have they been since the person has been missing? All that plays a part in whether I'll send trailing dogs or air-scenting dogs, or both. If the mission requires air-scent dogs, I want to get at least a half-dozen, if possible.

"Then I start telephoning handlers in the area and get them ready to go." Fran herself goes on an average of twenty missions a year. "Victims have ranged in age from eighteen months to one hundred and one years old," she says. "A missing child is always a high-priority search that commands the immediate response of all available search-team members, particularly the dog teams."

Barbara May, a Denver schoolteacher, is a member of SARDOC with her German shepherd, Sona. "If I were called out, I'd gather up my gear and food and water for Sona and myself," says Barbara, "and drive with her to the base camp that had been set up for the search. The people at base camp would include the local sheriff, the search manager, the emergency medical technicians or perhaps a doctor, and navigators. I'd report to the search manager, and when the searchers were divided into teams of three or four people, I would be assigned to a team.

"We might be searching for hours, maybe days. If the base camp was in an accessible place, the Red Cross or the Salvation Army might come with hot food for us.

"The outcome of the mission could be any of several possibilities—it's rare for search teams to come up with nothing. If we were truly lucky, we'd find the victim alive. However, out here in the mountains, it's more likely that we would find the body. And another possibility is that the mission would be called off because the object of the search walked out of the woods unaided or turned up somewhere and was never lost at all."

Thick brush, ground cover, and rock outcroppings in any type of wilderness or even countryside can completely obscure a missing person from a regular search team of human beings, but not from a good search dog. In Colorado, climbing casualties make dogs especially valuable.

"A few years ago, a twelve-year-old boy was hiking in rough terrain with his family when he disappeared," says Fran, who has experienced all the possible outcomes of a mission. "Two hundred searchers were looking for him everywhere. The trail the family had been hiking led along the top of a fifteen-hundred-foot cliff, but the searchers could not find any trace of the boy. Then, two different air-scent dogs, independent of each other, alerted at the same location. The terrain was so rugged that it was a full week before the searchers found the boy's body, in exactly the area below the cliff where the air-scent dogs had alerted."

As for a mission that turned out to be a false alarm, Fran tells of searching for a male jogger who had been reported missing. "One of my dogs was right on his track for some distance till it ended at a main road," she says. "The dog milled around trying to find the scent again, but that was it—nothing. This led the searchers to suspect that the guy might have hitched a ride to town, and that turned out to be the case."

And sometimes, happily, victims who are truly lost are found alive. Ann Wichmann tells of one instance when her dog, Logan, was a hero.

"We were called out to look for an antler hunter—someone who collects, usually as a hobby, the antlers that male deer shed in the spring before they grow new ones," Ann explains. "His vehicle and a cap had been found, which gave Logan his scent. Logan started trailing him along a path that other searchers assumed the man had taken, but after about half a mile, Logan left the trail and took off, air scent-ing. He simply picked up the guy's scent in the air and cut off a long loop of his trail by leading me about three-quarters of a mile straight to him. The man was very happy to be found!"

Less happy to be found are the illegal hunters in the park that Logan leads Ann to. Rangers are armed, but it is illegal for any visitors to carry firearms in the park. "What usually happens is that a picnicker or hiker sees someone heading into the woods carrying a rifle, tells us, and points out his vehicle," says Ann. "Logan will pick up the scent from the vehicle, and off we go. We catch the hunter in no time. If I were by myself, I could be walking around looking for him for hours, in danger of being mistaken for a deer and shot by mistake. The hunter, of course, is not thrilled to see us."

Fran Lieser recalls a time when Pockets was searching at a site where a dam had broken and it was feared campers might be missing. "Pockets alerted at a particular area where boulders had been piled up by the rushing water. The park ranger and other authorities had roped that area off because it wasn't safe—the rocks might start to slide. They insisted nobody was in there, and that the dog must be mistaken," Fran recalls. "But Pockets kept alerting, so I searched the area anyway. We found four engineers climbing around among the rocks, surveying the damage. In the confusion, nobody had known they were there.

"You learn to trust your dog," Fran continues. "Once Pockets and I were called out to search for a very elderly man who had been mushroom-hunting with his family and had gotten separated somehow. They had been looking all over for him for hours, and were frantic. Pockets picked up his trail and set off in a direction that led across fields en-closed by a series of barbed-wire fences. The family doubted that their relative could have climbed the fences, and after the fourth one, even I began to think Pockets must be wrong—an elderly person couldn't possibly have gotten over those fences.

"Well, Pockets was right. The old guy had not only climbed all those barbed-wire fences and gone all that distance, but he was very embarrassed at having been the object of a search. He never did admit he had been lost."

4
Deep Snow, Deep Water

Avalanche and Water Search Dogs

It was late March in the Sierra Mountains of California when the weather turned ugly. Snow had been falling hard and steadily for several days, building up, and winds gusted at 125 miles an hour. Vehicle accidents blocked mountain roads, ski areas closed down, and some people living on the slopes moved out of their homes.

At a ski area called Alpine Meadows, the highly experienced mountain manager working in the ski patrol office in the summit building was on the telephone and the radio with other authorities in the vicinity, trying to judge the possibility of an avalanche. He sent most of his employees home while he and several of his staff remained on duty.

Anna Conrad, a young woman who lived nearby and worked as a ski lift operator at Alpine Meadows, ignoring the danger, decided to ski from her home to the summit building with her friend Frank. When they arrived, they were soundly bawled out by the mountain manager for the extremely foolish thing they had done. That stern lecture was the last human voice Anna was to hear for a long time.

A few minutes later, Anna was in the locker room when an avalanche tore loose from the top of the mountain. Giant slabs of snow thundered down with a powerful, screaming

56

wind, burying everything in their path. Buildings at the ski area were blasted into the air. Under the force of the first shock wave, the summit building exploded, hurling occupants through the walls or under debris, many to their deaths.

Anna Conrad was thrown to the floor, unconscious. When she came to, she realized she was lying in a small space formed by a row of heavy wooden lockers that had fallen across a bench above her.

It was two hours before rescue teams and equipment, brought in by helicopters, snowmobiles, and tracked vehicles called snowcats, could begin to converge on the disaster site. Wreckage was spread over five acres of the mountain. The sheriff called for search dogs; two dogs and their handlers from a search-and-rescue outfit called WOOF responded.

The dogs, floundering through the huge snowdrifts and debris, eagerly alerted at several spots where equipment and other articles bearing human scent were found, as well as at spots where bodies were later uncovered. Searchers tried using probes—aluminum poles twelve to fifteen feet long—without success. Probes are widely used in searches for victims buried in snow. If a probe hits something soft like a body or a backpack, searchers know where to dig. But snow was still falling fast, and as darkness closed in, threat of a new avalanche sent all the rescuers out of the area.

In her tomb fifteen feet beneath the surface, Anna ate snow and put on layers of clothes that she was able to reach in the lockers that had fallen across her.

The next day, risking their own lives, ski patrols used explosives to control further avalanche slides, and got out of the area just ahead of another storm. For several days, whenever there was a break in the weather, searchers returned and worked frantically with dogs and equipment, but repeatedly they were driven off the mountain by fresh blizzards. Bodies were found, including that of Anna's friend Frank, but Anna Conrad and the mountain manager were still missing. One search dog team heard a dog whining in the

The scene at Alpine Meadows a few days after the avalanche. In the background is what's left of the summit building under which Anna Conrad was buried.

debris of the summit building, and rescuers uncovered a very frightened but unharmed German shepherd. She had been brought to Alpine Meadows for training and was in the dog room of the summit building when the avalanche hit.

On the third day, a German shepherd named Bridget alerted above Anna's burial place. Anna heard Bridget's handler, Roberta Huber, calling her, and she yelled back, but no one could hear her. Terror seized Anna as she heard footsteps crunching away in the snow, then silence. She had no idea how much time passed after that (later she learned it was two days). She knew she couldn't last much longer.

But Bridget and Roberta came back as soon as the weather cleared again. By now, the search area was contaminated with the many scents of searchers and equipment, but Bridget pawed and whined at the wreckage of the summit building where she had alerted before. Rescuers brought chain saws, shovels, and earth-moving equipment, working carefully so as not to cause more debris to collapse beneath them. They dug a shaft down into the snow and rubble and lowered Bridget down to tell them which direction to dig, left or right. All hands worked feverishly on the unlikely assumption that whoever the dog was alerting to was still alive. But again the weather drove everyone off the mountain.

At last, after five days trapped in her icy tomb, Anna was lifted out, alive and conscious. Bridget licked her face.

An hour later, the body of the mountain manager was found. Seven people had died at Alpine Meadows. Anna Conrad lost part of both feet, but she was given the rest of her life, thanks in large part to the brave dog from WOOF.

Recovering in the hospital, Anna is reunited with Bridget, the dog who saved her life, and Bridget's owner, Roberta Huber.

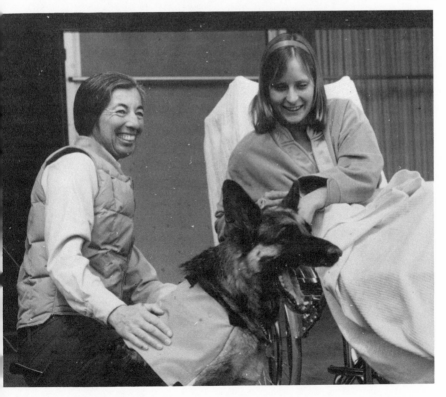

Avalanches

Avalanches occur frequently in the mountains of the American West. There are thousands every year, especially as lumber companies are allowed to cut down forests. Trees on the sides of mountains help prevent avalanches, but when a mountainside is stripped, there is nothing to prevent or stop the massive, deadly slides of snow.

Anna Conrad survived the Alpine Meadows avalanche initially because of several unlikely but lucky circumstances: She was in an air space provided by the lockers and bench that entombed her; she was able to get clothing to cover her; and she could eat snow to keep from dehydrating.

In truth, however, avalanche victims rarely make it. If they are caught in the open and buried under snow—and not under miraculously protective debris as Anna was—they smother in half an hour or less, depending on the density of the snow. Most of the time, rescuers, including avalanche dogs, find only bodies.

It is estimated that there are some 500 certified avalanche dogs in Europe. They succeed in many live rescues because they and their handlers are stationed at ski areas or nearby villages and can be at a disaster site, or mobilized to search for a missing skier, immediately. In smaller countries such as France and Switzerland, ski and snowshoe trails are closer to habitation, unlike the vast wilderness areas of the United States.

The mountains of the American West are spread over areas encompassing many states, and ski slopes and trails for other snow-related sports are often remote from towns. If our search-and-rescue dogs were used only for avalanche work, they would have to spend most of their time in training to keep their skills at peak efficiency. Also, during summer months, the snow on the mountains melts, and the dogs would have nothing to do but sit around forgetting their training.

Instead, dogs that belong to WOOF in California, to SAR-DOC in Colorado, and to many other similar American rescue organizations are trained for several types of wilderness and disaster searches. Many are also trained for avalanche search. When avalanches occur, those dogs are brought as quickly as possible, often by helicopter, to the disaster sites. In the United States it makes more sense to train dogs for multipurpose wilderness searches than to train them only for avalanche work.

Though after an avalanche the odds are against finding people alive, the search dogs do their best anyway because they know their job. Their handlers work on hope.

"Avalanche searches, even with certified avalanche dogs, are unpredictable," says Judy Chilen, who works as a member of the ski patrol at Vail, Colorado, and who with her Chesapeake Bay retriever, Chester, is a member of SARDOC. "Sometimes the dogs work just like in the book; other times they are ineffective.

"The first time I went out with Chester on a real search, we were looking for a skier. The man had told a friend he wanted to ski in a certain area, even though it had been roped off because there was danger of an avalanche. He planned to duck under the ropes, ski down, and meet his friend later. When he didn't show up, a search was organized, and I was called out. By that time it was eight or nine o'clock at night, and dark, and an avalanche had indeed occurred in the roped-off area. Chester alerted right away, but a probe didn't hit anything, and we were called off because of fresh avalanche danger.

"Next day, two other dogs and Chester alerted at the same place, and again a probe didn't find anything," Judy continues. "Rescuers continued to probe all around the place and eventually found the skier's body, about ten or twenty feet from where the dogs were alerting. I learned something from that: The scent of a person under snow may not rise to the surface directly above the body, but might take the line of least resistance, depending on the condition of the snow. In wet spring snow such as this, there were air pockets mixed with dense spots, and the vapor from the body traveled for several feet, emerging right where the dogs alerted.

"Another time, at Breckenridge, the avalanche dogs, including Chester, were ineffective. I never figured out why. Yet after an avalanche at Berthoud Pass, another handler and I were flown up four days later, as soon as it was safe, and it took the dogs two minutes to find the bodies."

Judy, who is married to a police officer and has two young children, practices with Chester regularly to keep up his certification for air-scenting as well as avalanche work. Why is she willing to be called out in all weathers, to struggle through freezing snow or rough terrain, when so often the reward is not a life saved but a body found?

"I like working with dogs, and I like helping people," she says. "You always hope to find someone alive, but even when you find a body, it is helpful to all concerned to know what happened. The victim's family and friends need to have the tragedy resolved, searchers need to know they no longer have to take risks or spend time in a needless search. And also, I love the challenge of the search."

Avalanche Training

In training a dog for avalanche search, it is one thing to bury a bundle of clothing in three feet of snow and then bring the dog to sniff the area searching for it. These exercises take place until the dog knows she is supposed to find the buried objects and digs eagerly in the snow to obtain them.

It is quite another thing to teach a dog to find a buried person. Before the dog can be fully trained and certified, live victims must be used repeatedly—people who volunteer to play the role of a victim and allow themselves to be buried under several feet of snow. This is dangerous. The reason nobody has died when buried in a training exercise is that it is done by professionals under very controlled circumstances. Nevertheless, the volunteer victim must have extremely steady nerves and plenty of faith in the dogs and handlers.

Methods of training dogs for avalanche search vary somewhat among rescue organizations, but the general techniques are similar. SARDOC uses the following system.

A practice slope is chosen and a trench or pit about three feet deep is dug in the snow for the volunteer to lie in. A small cave is hollowed out at the head of the trench to provide breathing space; this is reinforced so it won't collapse when the snow is heaped on to cover the trench. The victim is given a radio with which to communicate with the people on the ground above, and a radio person and two shovelers are assigned to be responsible for his or her life. Then the victim lies down in the trench.

The trench, when covered with snow, disappears, and the ground looks just like any other place on the practice slope. It can't be marked with flags because then the dog's handler would know where it is and unconsciously communicate this knowledge to the dog. But obviously, since somebody is being buried alive here, it is crucial that the exact spot be known. So before the trench is filled in with snow, its location is fixed by triangulating with a compass: A person takes a reading from two fixed, marked spots nearby (marked trees, for instance), and notes that the trench is at the point where the degree lines from the marked spots cross on the compass, forming the third point of a triangle. That way the trainers know precisely where the trench is, and it can be covered over with snow.

Now the dog and handler are brought to the scene. The dog goes to work; she has thirty minutes to find the person.

Before they can perform in a real avalanche search, all trained dogs must be certified by the search-and-rescue organization to which their handlers belong. For example, a SARDOC dog must pass a test based on the following procedures, abbreviated and paraphrased here.

In a training exercise, a dog alerts to a spot where a "victim" is buried under the snow.

The simulated avalanche slope will be at least 150 feet from top to bottom and 100 feet across. Two subjects (victims) plus a dummy made of clothing articles will be buried out of sight of the test team in moderate-depth snow of average density. After approximately ten minutes, handler and dog must approach and navigate rapidly and carefully despite radio interruptions and persons on the perimeter. When the dog indicates the first victim, she will be diverted and restarted while shovelers clear a shallow hole to eighteen inches. When the dog indicates the second victim, she will be diverted and placed at the first hole to test whether she will reindicate. If she digs accurately and positively, she will be permitted to fully recover that victim and receive her reward. The dog must locate both live victims within thirty minutes. She must show greater enthusiasm for the live victims than for the dummy.

If a dog can do all that to the satisfaction of the SARDOC evaluation committee, she becomes certified and can be called with her handler to use her keen sense of smell to find the bodies of victims in the snow—and maybe, some-day, a survivor. She probably offers the best chance the vic-tim has.

This is what an avalanche victim might see if he were lucky: rescuers digging him out and the trained dog who alerted to him.

Water Training

On a wilderness search or even a disaster search, a search-and-rescue dog often stands a fairly good chance of finding a victim alive. In fact, when they are climbing through the rubble at a disaster site at which there may be numerous victims, some dogs will even lead their handlers to live people first.

However, while there is little chance of finding victims alive after an avalanche, there is generally no chance in water. Though it is a sad thing for the handler and other searchers to find the body of a drowned person, especially a child, it is important to the victim's family to resolve the question of what happened to their loved one. And as in any search, it is also important to the police and other searchers to find the body, so the search can be ended and the manpower directed to other jobs. Sometimes, when the facts of a drowning are known, safety measures are enacted to protect others in the future.

Dogs trained for water search have proved to have a very high success rate in finding drowning victims. The dogs will eagerly try to find a body under water because they know that's what their handlers want of them, they know that's their job, they know they'll be rewarded for doing it, and they are proud of themselves.

Training methods vary somewhat among different search-and-rescue dog outfits. In one part of the United States, water searches may take place in deep, cold mountain lakes; in another place, ponds and streams may be the sites of drownings. But in general, training methods proceed along the following lines, as described by Marian Hardy of DOGS-East, who is also an officer in the National Association for Search and Rescue (NASAR), which most search-and-rescue dog groups belong to.

"For water search, the dog can usually search from a boat,

In a water training exercise, Marian Hardy's dog, Kerry, an expert search-and-rescue dog, sometimes enters the water and pulls the "victim" to shore. ED JOHNSON

from the shore, or in certain circumstances from the water while swimming. There are really three parts to the training— to teach the dog to detect human scent coming from under water, to ride in and work from some sort of boat, and possibly to work while swimming.

"The preferred method for introducing a dog to human scent coming from under water is to have a diver wearing scuba gear enter the water, out of sight of the dog, and linger at a spot several feet below the surface. When the dog passes downwind of the diver's scent, she will alert in some fashion—by whining, by barking, even by pawing or biting at the water. In a boat, she might scratch at the bottom of the boat or try to jump overboard. On shore, she might enter

the water and swim toward the spot where the scent is ema-
nating from the water. The handler learns to recognize her
dog's alert and signals the diver to surface. Together they reward the dog, thus reinforcing the dog's initiative to alert to
human scent, even from under water.

*Logan alerts to a human scent rising from underwater. The diver
surfaces and Logan is praised for his find.*

"Since divers may not always be available for training sessions, additional practice can be done using recently worn clothing weighted and put under water for the dogs to detect.

"Both the handler and the dog must learn to be comfortable in various kinds of small boats, such as canoes, rowboats, Zodiacs, and rubber rafts, and on various types of water, such as rivers with currents and rapids, as well as lakes and ponds. The dogs also learn to walk on tippy, slippery, or bouncing surfaces and not to jump off when something starts to move under them. They are taught to climb up and down ladders, walk on narrow logs over water, and in general to trust that their handlers will only ask them to do things that are safe.

"Though you don't send a dog into flooded rivers or streams, or into rapids or any body of water with unknown hazards, it's a good idea for the dog to learn to be comfortable in the water and be a strong swimmer. Most dogs naturally take to water, others have to be coaxed in at first and to practice swimming until they do it easily. The dog's handler plays with the dog at a lake or pond, throwing a stick or ball in the water for her to fetch. The training is fun and a game, but even so, not all dogs really want to swim. One of our dogs hates swimming and won't do it for pleasure, but when she alerts to someone under water during a search, she'll enter the water and swim—a pretty good alert!"

Marian has collected reports on water searches from over 100 search-and-rescue dog organizations nationwide. It is not uncommon for dogs to find victims in water as deep as eighty feet, she says. And while nobody is certain how long a submerged victim's body produces enough scent for a dog to detect, Marian knows of a documented case in which a dog in California found a body in a river after 192 days.

"Because of water currents and depth, dogs can't always pinpoint the exact spot where a body is to be found," Marian says. "But their alerts will tell divers which area to

Some dogs have to learn to like going in water. One teaching method in training a dog for water search is to play fetch with him at a lake.

search. And in addition to actually alerting to the victim, one of the most important contributions of dogs during a water search is to show where the victim isn't—the dogs can 'clear' large areas of lakes and miles of rivers, so the underwater divers and dragging operators don't have to search those areas. Dogs, of course, can only alert to the presence of a body; it must then be recovered by other means, such as divers or dragging operations."

Searchers must be able to take into consideration such forces as water currents and wind. If, for example, a dog is searching for a lost child whose trail ends at the side of a river, that is probably the spot where the child fell in, though not necessarily where the body will be found. The dog may have to search considerably farther downstream to the area where the body is more likely to be before she can be expected to alert.

Marian believes that if water search dogs were brought quickly to the site of a suspected drowning in extremely cold water, some victims might be rescued alive because of a phenomenon called the mammalian diving reflex, or MDR.

The MDR is an involuntary response that occurs when someone is suddenly submerged in very cold water. Breathing stops, the pulse slows down, the larynx shuts, keeping water out of the lungs. The brain reduces its need for oxygen, and blood is directed away from muscles and toward the heart and the brain. The body is in a state of lifeless suspension that can enable a human being to survive an amazingly long time, perhaps hours, under water.

In the past, people pulled from the water in this state were often assumed to be drowned. But since the MDR has become known, efforts at resuscitation have revived a number of presumed drowning victims.

The colder the water, the better the chance that the mammalian diving reflex will keep a person alive long enough to be rescued. And because trained dogs have such a high success rate at locating bodies under water, Marian reasons, it would be a good idea for them to be brought in immediately at sites with very cold water, such as mountain lakes. Lives might be saved, which is the goal of all search-and-rescue people.

5 "Find It!"

Narcotics Detector Dogs

"We were making a routine check of luggage coming off a plane from the Caribbean when Mojo suddenly alerted to a stylish little duffel bag," says Sue Rupchis. Sue was a canine enforcement officer with the United States Customs Service, working at John F. Kennedy International Airport in New York with her trained dog.

"The passengers were mostly people returning from vacations. Mojo was up on the luggage carousel outside the airport building where the bags are unloaded from the cart that carries them from the plane. The suitcases are laid flat so the narcotics detector dogs can jump from one to another on the moving carousel, sniffing as their weight expels scent from within the cases. Mojo was interested in that small duffel bag. We followed it inside to the baggage claim area and saw it picked up by a respectable-looking man in his forties, not at all the type that people expect drug smugglers to look like.

"We hung back and let the guy get in line to go through Customs. When his bag was opened and searched, nothing looked suspicious at first. But fortunately, the Customs inspector picked two cans out of the toilet articles kit—one labeled antiperspirant and one hair spray—and examined them.

They turned out to be full of hashish. The guy had drilled holes in the sides of the cans, poured out the contents, filled the cans with hash, soldered the holes shut, and pasted little price tags over the sealed holes. He had gone to a lot of trouble to bring in those two pounds of hash. And was he surprised at getting caught!

"Smugglers often try to conceal drugs in containers that they think will mask the odor—coffee cans, perfume bottles, spice cans, and the like. But Mojo wasn't fooled. He detected the hash right through the sealed cans that had held scented substances."

Trained dogs have been used for narcotics detection by the Customs Service since 1970. There are 169 of them today, stationed at the borders, airports, and seaports where vehicles, planes, and ships enter the United States from foreign countries.

Mojo's hit that evening was not unusual. In fact, it was routine. The dogs easily intercept the so-called soft drugs such as marijuana and hashish, even from several hundred yards away if conditions are right. Though hard drugs are more difficult for them, they catch plenty of cocaine, heroin, and even opium. They have been known to alert to amphetamines and barbiturates. In 1987, in 3,854 seizures, the dog-and-handler teams intercepted a total of over 570,000 pounds of cocaine, heroin, opium, hashish, marijuana, and packets of pills, with a street value of more than $844 million.

"We've heard that there's a bounty out for Customs dogs at the Mexican border," says Steve Failla, a supervisor of fourteen canine enforcement teams at Kennedy Airport.

Dogs and Handlers

What breed makes the best Customs Service dog? Steve Failla thinks that sporting dogs—retrievers, pointers, and Weimaraners, for example, or mixed breeds of sporting-dog parentage—have superior potential for drug detection work.

Steve's dog, Buffy, is a yellow Labrador retriever, Mojo is a black Labrador mixed breed, and Beto, the dog that found the cocaine in Chapter 1, is a golden retriever.

The dogs may be male or female; the females are spayed, and the males may or may not be neutered, depending on temperament. They don't live with their handlers; when they're not working, the dogs sleep and eat in commercial kennels. However, when the dogs retire, their handlers usually keep them. Buffy is nine years old, "about ready for retirement," says Steve. "And I'm going to keep him. He'll live at home and be our family pet."

While some of the dogs are privately donated, a cheerful fact about Customs Service dogs is that most of them are selected from animal shelters. Sometimes a humane society will notify the Customs Detector Dog Training Center at Front Royal, Virginia, when a likely dog is surrendered to the shelter by its owner. But several times a year, instructors from the training center visit animal shelters throughout the United States looking for young, suitable dogs.

Is the dog between one and three years old and in good health? Does it have a good temperament and seem intelligent? Is it self-confident and energetic? Will it retrieve and play tug-of-war with a towel? These are among the questions that the instructor has in mind when evaluating a dog.

"Once I was walking down the aisles of cages at an animal shelter bouncing a ball," recalls Sue Rupchis. "Customs likes dogs who will watch the ball rather than the person. I saw a nice-looking golden retriever who was interested in the ball, but when I took him out of the cage, he became more attentive to me than to the ball, like a dog who would make a wonderful pet. But there was another dog, a medium-sized mixed breed, in the cage with him who was eyeing the ball, and when I took him out, he didn't pay any attention to me—he played fetch with that ball like crazy. He became a great narcotics detector dog."

If a dog passes all the initial tests, he or she goes to the training center, is evaluated again, and if accepted, enters a class and is assigned to a handler.

When the canine enforcement program began, Steve Failla was one of the first handlers. All the early handlers were career military men with canine experience; Steve's erect bearing and his air of confident authority suggest his army background. Now, however, to become a canine enforcement officer (CEO), it's best to have a college degree or associate degree, or to be already working in some branch of the Customs Service.

About 10 percent of the officers today are women. Sue Rupchis has a college degree in animal behavior and has worked at a zoo; when she joined the canine program, she was hired to do kennel work, then rose through the ranks to CEO. Barbara Wilson, another CEO at Kennedy Airport, had had two years of college and was doing administrative work in the Customs Service when she learned about the canine program. She applied and was accepted.

Applicants for canine enforcement are interviewed and evaluated at a regional office, then go to Front Royal. They must be prepared to work in all kinds of weather and at all hours; they must like dogs and not mind working in rough or dirty conditions. They are evaluated throughout their training, both with their dogs and in written exams.

In addition to learning to handle their dogs in Customs work, they are taught law and the use of firearms. When working, canine enforcement officers are armed. While drug smugglers arriving on planes are unlikely to be carrying concealed guns, people meeting them might be. Steve says he has had to pull his gun only once. "I had detained a passenger for questioning when a man who had come to meet him reached inside his shirt," he explains. "I reacted automatically, though fortunately it turned out not to be necessary."

However, CEOs with their dogs sometimes assist local narcotics agents in raids. In the course of following a package of drugs to its ultimate destination in order to arrest the seller, the officers and agents may use the dogs in searching a residence.

"Mojo and I were once called out to assist local police officers in a drug arrest at a house," says Sue. "After the police arrested the people in the house and brought them out, Mojo and I started into the house to find the evidence. 'There's a cat in the house,' someone warned, thinking Mojo might be distracted by the cat's scent and not try to find the drugs. But Mojo went about his business and quickly alerted to the back of a closet—in fact, he was pawing and trying to eat the back wall. The officers took the closet apart and didn't find anything. But then someone noticed that this closet shared a wall with a closet in another room. And in that one they found over four pounds of cocaine. Mojo hadn't paid any attention to the cat, who was discovered under a bed. It's as if he had said, "I'm not in this house to find cats, I'm here to find narcotics.' "

Training a Narcotics Detector Dog

Let's follow a typical dog whom we'll call Hunter through his twelve weeks at the Training Center at Front Royal.

Hunter is a yellow Labrador, two years old, who was chosen at an animal shelter in Chicago. He has passed his physical and other evaluation tests and has been assigned to a handler who is also in training. The dog and the handler will go through the course together.

Hunter's handler is a young man named Joe. Though Hunter has to share his handler with one other dog, he quickly bonds with him, trying to please him and win praise from him. At the center, he and the other dog live in the kennel, but work only with their handler. For the first two weeks, Joe learns how to handle and care for his two dogs, and they get to know each other.

Hunter starts his training by learning to detect marijuana and hashish. Joe begins by teaching him to find and retrieve his play object, which is a tightly rolled-up towel with a little bundle of marijuana or hashish tied in it. Joe hides the towel in tall grass, or in a room, and when Hunter finds it, his handler praises him and plays with him. Hunter learns to associate the scent of the drugs with his beloved towel. When Joe eventually withdraws the towel and hides only one of the drugs, telling Hunter to "Find it!" Hunter is happy to obey because as soon as he finds the scented object he's looking for, Joe throws the rolled-up towel in front of him and they have a game of tug-of-war with it.

By the end of six weeks, Hunter has become adept at finding anything with the odor of marijuana or hashish on it, because that means Joe will praise him and play with him. He is evaluated by the instructors and passes, meaning he is certified for detecting soft drugs.

Now Hunter graduates to learning to detect hard drugs—heroin and cocaine. The training procedure is the same, but these substances are more difficult to detect. Joe's other dog cannot reliably find them, and flunks out. Because he is a perfectly nice dog, one of the kennel workers wants him and takes him home to be a family pet. Some dogs who can't progress to hard-drug detection but who show promise are given a second chance and kept longer at the first level of training. However, most who are having trouble either go to homes that are found for them or are returned to their original owners or humane society shelters.

Hunter's training becomes tough. He has learned to detect both soft and hard drugs by themselves, but now the narcotics are mixed with other scents of the kind that smugglers hope will throw the dogs off—tobacco, coffee, toiletries, spices, perfume, anything with a distinctive odor. Not only must Hunter learn to discriminate among the thousands of different odors that meet his sensitive nose, but Joe has to learn to recognize Hunter's signals. Since Hunter will investigate many scents that are interesting to him, Joe must be able to tell if Hunter is just sniffing from curiosity or if he is following his nose to a target substance. When Hunter and the other dogs still in training find the odor they've learned will bring them praise and a game, they scratch and bite excitedly at the container in which it is concealed.

Joe and Hunter graduate from the training center and are assigned as a team to a post—an international airport, shipping port, or border crossing, usually in the region where the handler applied. If a handler happens to finish with both of the dogs he started with, he gets to choose the dog he likes better, and the second dog is kept for other Customs work, or repeats the course with another handler.

When Joe and Hunter arrive at their post, Joe gives Hunter a few weeks of additional training to accustom the dog to his actual working environment. Then their supervisor assigns them to a schedule, and the team goes to work.

The Working Team

Steve Failla and Sue Rupchis are searching a cargo area with Sue's dog, Mojo. Steve has arranged for a package of narcotics to be hidden in one of the crates, because the dogs need daily training in order to keep up their skill and motivation. This is called task-related training, because it simulates the dog's regular work. (If a dog were given a training session in a place other than his daily work environment—a building interior, for example—it would be termed non-task-related training.)

Mojo is eagerly sniffing the crates, boxes, and cartons, jumping up on them, nosing the cracks between them. Mojo is by temperament a busybody, which is one characteristic of a good narcotics detector dog. "Find it, Mojo!" Sue repeats again and again to encourage the dog.

Suddenly Mojo zeroes in on a carton, pulls it away from the others, and proceeds to try to tear it apart. "Good dog!" exclaims Sue, throwing Mojo's rolled-up towel in front of him, which the dog gleefully grabs and begins to romp with. Mojo's reward is a quick game of tug-of-war with his handler. When he gets to relax, Mojo is a clown.

In a narcotics search, Officer Sue Rupchis directs Mojo to inspect a crate that was just unloaded from a freighter.

"Mojo's reaction was typical of a dog when he makes a find," explains Steve. "We then divert him from the carton or suitcase so he won't destroy the package of narcotics that we need for evidence.

"But I remember once when a dog overdid his job," Steve continues. "I was with a couple of canine enforcement teams down in Texas checking cars that were lined up to cross the border from Mexico. We were unloading the dogs from their traveling cages in our station wagons when one dog suddenly put his nose in the air, sniffed, slipped his leash, and raced down the line of cars for several hundred yards. We started after him, of course, but within seconds he came tearing back to us, very proud of himself, with something in his mouth. He took it straight to his handler. It was a whole brick of marijuana.

"But we had no idea where he'd found it! There was no point in going down the line interrogating drivers to try and

discover which car the dog had taken it from, as if anybody would admit it. Can you imagine a uniformed Customs
officer saying to a driver, 'Pardon me, but is this your
marijuana?' and the guy saying, 'Oh yes, Officer, I was just
bringing it into the United States!' So we simply praised
the dog for his hit and went to work."

Sue tells a story of an unusual reaction of Mojo's during a
luggage search at JFK. "Mojo was on the moving carousel,
jumping from one bag to the other, when suddenly he simply
sat down on one, heading right into the terminal. I thought,
'Why on earth is he riding this suitcase?' so I pulled him off
and followed the suitcase inside. We really got suspicious
when nobody claimed it. So we took it into a Customs office, where it was opened. It was literally filled with marijuana—one hundred pounds of it! I figured out why Mojo
had sat down. The scent was so overpowering to him that
he gave an abnormal response. In training, CEOs are taught

*In one of the huge cargo sheds at John F. Kennedy Airport, Beto
detects a narcotic scent and tries to tear the carton apart.*

At a checkpoint on the Mexican border, a Border Patrol dog named Brando is on duty to detect not only drugs but also illegal aliens being smuggled into the U.S. A.J. KMIECIK/THE PRESS-ENTERPRISE

to always investigate a dog's abnormal response, as well as his usual responses, and this one paid off.

"Probably the suitcase was never intended to come through Customs, where it would stand such a big chance of being discovered. It was undoubtedly what is called a 'whip job': A deal had been made with someone out on the field to remove the suitcase surreptitiously, either in the plane or from the baggage cart, and spirit it away before it ever reached the terminal building. Something must have gone wrong with this whip job."

Generally, only luggage and cargo arriving at United States ports from foreign countries are searched by Customs. Under our laws, a person, car, home, luggage, or anything else within the United States usually cannot be searched without a search warrant issued by a judge. However, sometimes the police receive a tip on someone or something arriving on a domestic flight from another American city—the person has been arrested for big-time drug dealing in the past, for example, or he's under suspicion for some other reason involving narcotics. Then a Customs narcotics detector dog may be brought to examine the person's luggage or packages on arrival. And if the dog alerts, the owner can be detained for a reasonable time while local police obtain a search warrant from a judge. The trained dog's alert, coupled with the tip, is considered "probable cause," a legal term for circumstances under which a judge will sign a search warrant so luggage or packages can be opened and examined without the owner's consent.

Also, in similar cases when there is reasonable suspicion, a car can be detained within the United States long enough to bring a dog to search it, and if the dog alerts, a judge will issue a search warrant.

Customs dogs do not search people because the animals are trained to give what's called an aggressive alert. As Beto, Mojo, Buffy, and the other narcotics dogs demonstrated, they paw and bite at the containers. But occasionally, when the dogs are searching a car at a border crossing, one may alert to people.

"We'll have the passengers waiting a little distance away while the dogs work the car," Steve explains. "Suddenly a dog will turn his attention from the car, sniff the air, and look at or start toward the passengers. The Customs officers then search the passengers too—not just their pockets but their bodies, in case anyone has packets of drugs taped to his back, thighs, or legs. In fact, Customs officers are trained to notice when people are likely to have narcotics taped to their bodies just by the subtle changes in the way they walk and move. They catch a lot of smugglers that way."

Sue and Mojo also worked at the seaport at Newark, New Jersey, with her supervisor there, Herbert Herter, and his dog, Adam, a German short-haired pointer. They made routine searches of ships—the crew's quarters, the kitchen, the cargo hatches, perhaps even the engine room.

At the Newark, New Jersey, seaport Sue and Mojo approach a freighter that has just arrived. They must search it for drugs.

Drugs are rarely hidden in the crew's cabins but are sometimes concealed in the engine room. Mojo must ignore all the many normal smells and concentrate on trying to find substances he is trained to detect.

Most cargo shipped today is containerized—packed into metal containers that are from twenty to forty feet long, about six feet wide, and ten feet tall. The dogs and handlers also work the container fields, the huge piers where the enormous containers are unloaded. The containers are lifted from the ships by machine and set onto flatbed trucks that are then driven to ramps where the dogs can check around the sides. The double doors at the back of the containers are opened so the dogs can sniff the back of the cargo. If there are narcotics hidden in any of the cargo inside, the dogs will most likely detect it and alert.

Mojo alone made thirty narcotics seizures in one year. If our country has not been very successful in its war on drugs, it is not the fault of these intelligent and hardworking animals and their handlers.

Officer Herbert Herter and his dog, Adam, check out containers that have just been unloaded onto a pier. In cool weather, odors from the stacked containers tend to drift downward. If Adam alerts, the upper containers will be lifted down by a crane and inspected.

6
The Beagle Brigade

Department of
Agriculture Dogs

The passengers trooped into the terminal building at John F. Kennedy International Airport and milled around among the hundreds of other people whose flights had landed before theirs. They were all trying to keep track of children, manage their bundles and hand luggage, and locate which of many carousels would bring in their baggage from the planes. Then they would have to line up for Customs inspection, at which point their bags would be opened and searched, and they would have to declare whatever they were bringing from abroad.

The scene was one of noisy confusion. There were Americans coming home from business trips or vacations, foreigners arriving on business or to visit friends or relatives in America, and people hoping to settle here. All had endured long, tiring journeys from Europe, Africa, the Caribbean, or South America, and they were anxious to collect their belongings, have their bags inspected by the Customs officers without any problems, and continue on their way to their ultimate destinations.

Suddenly, passengers waiting for their baggage noticed a little dog moving among them, a perky, short-legged brown and white hound wearing a green coat. Many people smiled;

Jackpot checks out a suitcase as his handler, Officer Hal Fingerman, questions an incoming airline passenger.

some looked puzzled. Children were fascinated; some squealed and reached out to pet the dog. This was Jackpot, an employee of the United States Department of Agriculture, who was not there just to look cute—he was working. Leading him was his handler, Hal Fingerman, an officer in the Department of Agriculture's Plant Protection and Quarantine canine program.

Jackpot's job was to screen luggage and packages for the substances he had been trained to detect: food and plants from abroad that are prohibited from being brought into the country. Whenever he picked up the scent of one of the illegal foodstuffs or other products forbidden by the Department of Agriculture, Jackpot quietly sat down, a signal to Hal that there was something to investigate.

Within minutes of coming to work among the passengers this afternoon, Jackpot sniffed curiously at a suitcase on the floor beside a young man holding a child in his arms. Jackpot sat down and looked expectantly up at Hal.

When he detects the smell of food or plant material, Jackpot alerts by sitting down.

"Do you have any fruit?" asked Hal. The man smiled and shook his head. "Do you speak English?" Hal asked. Again, the man just smiled. Hal tried the question in several languages. Getting nowhere, he checked the man's declaration card, on which passengers are supposed to indicate what they are bringing with them from abroad. The man had marked "No" beside the question about food.

Hal asked to look in the suitcase. Sorting through the contents, he discovered an eggplant, a bag of currants, and an orange, and checking further, a small plant with its roots in soil and wrapped in plastic. Slipping Jackpot a treat, Hal marked a green A on the man's declaration card—a signal to the Customs officer that an agriculture officer should search the man's luggage and remove all illegal agricultural products.

"Most people answer 'No' on their declaration cards," says Hal. "Sometimes they may honestly think that the rule doesn't apply to the pear they were given for lunch on the plane in midocean, or to a keepsake such as one little twig from a tree in the yard of the home where they grew up.

"But usually they are trying to get away with something. We have found fruits and vegetables tucked out of sight in shoes, sewn into coat linings, or carried in tobacco pouches. And as for meat, we've found meat concealed in baby strollers, even wrapped in perfume-soaked rags to disguise its odor. The lengths people will go to, to bring in contraband! I'll never forget one case when a woman came along whose luggage was clean, but Jackpot kept alerting to her. Customs had her taken into a private room and searched by a female employee, and it turned out she had sausages sewn into cloth belts that were wrapped around her body under her clothes.

"And the arguments they give us are amazing," Hal adds. " 'Meat?' somebody will say, 'I thought you meant cake.' One lady claimed her ham sandwich wasn't food because she wasn't eating it at the moment."

In the course of an hour, Jackpot's hits included apples,

A carton of illegal prickly pears did not get by Jackpot's trained nose.

nuts, lemons, limes, figs, some plants, and the innards of a steer. Why is our Department of Agriculture so interested in preventing food, plants, and animal products from entering the United States? Because foodstuffs and plants from other countries might be carrying viruses, bacteria, or pests (insects and the like) that could infect our crops and livestock. Certain dangerous fruit flies, moths, and beetles, viruses of animal infections such as hoof-and-mouth disease, and plant diseases with names like rust, blackleg, and canker have devastated whole agricultural regions in the past, before the present laws were passed. It takes only one infected orange, sausage, or plant to cause millions of dollars' worth of damage.

Some products are illegal no matter what country they are coming from; others are illegal only from countries where agricultural pests or diseases are known to be prevalent. For example, certain flower bulbs would be okay if they came from the Netherlands but not from Italy. Fresh fruits can be brought in from Jamaica but not from other countries. And in a few instances, some products can enter the United States at certain ports but not at others. Officer Hal Fingerman must remember a long list of prohibitions and exceptions.

"Besides food and plants, Jackpot has alerted to some pretty weird things. For instance, we confiscated a huge bird's nest somebody wanted to bring in," Hal continues. "That nest was constructed of mud, twigs, and leaves that could easily have been filled with viruses, bacteria, and insect eggs that could hatch and possibly wipe out a million dollars' worth of crops. What we do here has an impact on the food everybody in the country eats. Suppose, for example, all the orange trees in the Southeast were killed—growers would go broke, people would be out of work, and the price of oranges would go so high that hardly anybody could afford to buy them.

This mound of illegal edibles is the result of a typical day's work for Jackpot and Hal.

"Jackpot has even found birds, both dead and alive, that people were smuggling in. Irresponsible pet shops in the United States support many busy smugglers who deal in exotic birds. Some endangered species are being decimated by poachers who capture the birds and sell them to the smugglers. Not only that, but the birds might be carrying contagious avian diseases that could kill our own wild birds, and even chickens, for miles around."

The need for modern quarantine regulations gave rise to the present system of inspections at all ports of entry into the United States. Today, there are about 1,000 Department of Agriculture officers on duty at more than eighty ports who form the first line of defense against the organisms that could damage American agriculture. They inspect the baggage of some 300 million travelers a year; in one recent year, they confiscated approximately 200,000 products that were diseased or infested with harmful parasites.

In 1984, the Department of Agriculture launched an experiment in the use of trained scent detector dogs to assist the officers on duty. It started with two dogs who were stationed at the international airports in New York and Los Angeles. These dogs quickly proved so expert at their jobs that within two years the canine program was made permanent.

At first, the dogs were of various breeds, and often, like the narcotics detector dogs, worked behind the scenes on the carousels that carried luggage from the baggage carts into the passenger terminal. But it became apparent that the program would be most practical if the dogs worked among the passengers in the terminal waiting to go through Customs with their packages and hand luggage. So it was decided to use small, friendly dogs that would not frighten people—dogs such as beagles, who have good noses for scenting and are smart and nonthreatening. That's how the program came to be called the Beagle Brigade.

Today, the Department of Agriculture beagles work not only in New York, Los Angeles, and San Francisco but in

The Department of Agriculture decided to use small, friendly beagles such as Jackpot, who would not frighten people.

Miami, Atlanta, Chicago, and Seattle, too; others now in training will be assigned to other airports around the country in the future. In doing their jobs to protect American agriculture, the dogs also demonstrate to the public that the agricultural quarantine laws are to be taken seriously. The beagles make correct hits more than 80 percent of the time.

The dogs are male or female, chosen from animal shelters or privately donated. Their working life is eight to ten years, and when they retire, the last handlers to work with them get to keep them as pets if they like; otherwise homes are found for them. "I'll keep Jackpot myself, if possible," says Hal. "If my living situation is such that I can't, I'll choose a very good home for him."

Four-year-old Jackpot, who is part beagle and part basset hound, was given to the program by a private donor. He shares his job with another beagle, Sam, who works with another handler when Jackpot is off duty. Sam was found wandering on the street one day by an animal control officer; when nobody claimed him, the officer offered him to the Beagle Brigade. Hal, who coordinates all the canine programs on the East Coast, says two additional beagles are expected soon at Kennedy Airport.

Training

The first dogs of the Beagle Brigade were trained at Lackland Air Force Base in San Antonio, Texas, along with the handlers who would be working with them. At Lackland, the United States Department of Defense operates the largest training facility for dogs in the country: About 300 to 350 dogs are there at any given time, learning scent detection and other work for many branches of the federal government.

One of the first handlers in the Beagle Brigade program was Hal. Looking back, he says, "It was really funny—here were three hundred huge German shepherds, some of whom were being trained to attack, and then here we were with eight cute little friendly beagles." Now the beagles have their own training facilities in Miami and San Francisco.

"Our dogs are taught to give a passive response when they detect one of the target substances," explains Hal. "That means they learn to signal by sitting down, instead of by jumping, barking, or attacking the container that has the foodstuff in it. We don't want dogs tearing people's luggage apart; we just want them to alert us when they scent something.

"We teach a dog by first putting a little piece of meat in a box, and setting that box out among a lot of empty boxes. We lead the dog among the boxes, and when he finds the one with the meat in it, we teach him to respond by sitting down. When he sits, he's rewarded instantly. Then the dog graduates to scent discrimination. We hide meat in with other things—clothing, leather, bread, candy, anything with a distinguishing scent—and go through the same procedure.

And finally we leave out the meat and progress to citrus fruits such as mangoes, oranges, lemons, limes, and the like. We give him a treat every time he sits for them, so that he comes to associate those scents with a reward.

"Eventually we cut down on the food rewards and substitute praise and pats some of the time. The dog knows he will get something he likes for doing his job."

Training is eight to ten weeks for dogs and handlers together.

People working in Plant Protection and Quarantine must have at least a bachelor of science degree, usually in biology or agricultural science. "And for the canine program, they should also have some canine experience," adds Hal, who joined the program with a degree in animal science and some hands-on experience as a dog groomer.

Working

Jackpot, at work in the crowded arrivals building, sniffs at a bag and sits down. This time it is a large tote bag belonging to a young woman.

"Are you carrying any food in your bag?" asks Officer Hal Fingerman.

"Yes," replies the woman, holding out her declaration card. "I have a Dutch cheese and some chocolate." And she shows Hal a large, hard cheese and several bars of Belgian chocolate.

"Thank you," says Hal politely, and moves on with Jackpot.

Many foods—candy, cookies, jams, most nuts, coffee, tea, hard processed cheeses, wine, and olive oil among them— are permitted, and sometimes Jackpot sits down when he detects a product that turns out to be legal. It's up to Hal to distinguish between them.

"Once Jackpot alerted to a guy from Italy who had arrived to run in the New York City marathon with only a pair of sneakers, a T-shirt, and a big bag of chestnuts in the shell, which are illegal. It seemed like an odd choice of items to bring to another country, and I felt sort of sorry for him when I took the chestnuts away," Hal recalls. "Later, when I saw the list of winning runners in the newspaper, I noticed his name among the top twenty, and I was glad for him."

On occasion, half a day may go by without Jackpot's discovering any illegal food, plant, or animal products. When that happens, Hal puts some in a dummy suitcase and leaves it where Jackpot can find it, just to keep up the dog's skill and interest.

In rare instances, Hal and Jackpot have been attacked in the line of duty by passengers who were angry at being caught trying to smuggle illegal products. Jackpot has been stepped on and kicked, and once a child threw a lighted firecracker under his nose. "One time a lady got so mad when I took a mango from her that she took out a squeeze bottle of mustard and hosed me down with it," Hal recalls.

Every hour and a half, Hal gives Jackpot a break, taking him outside where he can trot around the restricted parking lot behind the terminal building, while Hal keeps an eye on him. Jackpot doesn't seem to tire easily from his work.

Jackpot gets a chance to run and play on his frequent breaks.

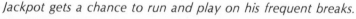

"Sometimes he'll put his nose in the air and run the whole length of the terminal to make a hit," says Hal proudly. "The machine hasn't yet been invented that's as sensitive as a dog's nose."

7
"Show Me!"

Explosives and
Arson Detector Dogs

A fire had gutted a factory just outside New Haven, Connecticut. The products manufactured there had been made of wood, so there was literally nothing left of them, and not much of the building either. The police suspected that the fire had been set deliberately, but they could find no evidence of arson in the charred debris.

After any fire of suspicious origin, the authorities always look for objects that might have contained an accelerant—a flammable substance such as gasoline, kerosene, paint remover, lacquer thinner, and the like—which arsonists use to start fires. If the authorities investigating a fire discover rags in odd places, for instance, or charring on the floor in a deliberate pattern, they might have the rags or floorboards tested in a laboratory for the presence of an accelerant.

But in the case of this factory, there was almost nothing left to take to the laboratory to test. At least, that's what the fire fighters and police thought.

Then someone suggested bringing Mattie to the scene; maybe she could find something. Mattie arrived on the end of a leash, for she is a black Labrador retriever belonging to the Connecticut State Police Canine Unit. Mattie is an arson specialist. She started sniffing through the wreckage of the factory and very soon alerted just inside the blistered door frame of the building. Bits of the burned door were tested for accelerant. Mattie was right, and a former employee of the factory who had a grudge against it was arrested. He confessed to setting the fire and went to jail.

The Connecticut State Police Canine Unit, established fifty-four years ago, trains and provides dog-and-handler teams for search and patrol work, and also for drug and explosives detection. But so far, Mattie is one of a kind, presumably unique in the United States and perhaps in the world. Sweet tempered and smart, Mattie has been taught to detect the odors of seventeen different chemicals.

"We believe she's more accurate than the devices designed for arson detection," says Trooper Doug Lancelot, one of Mattie's handlers. A problem with accelerant-detection instruments is that they don't differentiate between chemicals in synthetic materials that are normally released by fire, and the same chemicals used in accelerants. So the instruments often give false readings. But Mattie's nose is trained to single out those chemicals when used in accelerants.

In the year since she has been working, Mattie has been brought to the scene of some fifty fires, and has detected evidence of arson in more than half.

Mattie once found evidence of arson when she wasn't even at a fire site. A blaze had broken out in a high school, and the student who admitted setting it had been arrested, but the police wanted to substantiate his confession with evidence to use in court. The boy told them he had used gasoline to start the fire and had spilled some on his pants, but when the police went to his house to seize them as evidence, they had already been washed.

Nevertheless, the boy's clean pants were shown to Mattie on the outside chance that she might be able to detect the gasoline. She sniffed them over, then alerted with the response she had been taught. The pants smelled only of detergent to human noses, but not to Mattie's nose.

When the plan for training a dog for arson detection was first discussed, there was concern that the commotion and the acrid odors at a fire scene might distract the animal. But each time she was taken to a fire site, Mattie just went to work without paying any attention to the noise and activity around her.

Another worry was that the dog might be exposed to the danger of smoke inhalation, or step on hot embers or broken glass. Boots were bought for Mattie, but she hated them so much that finally it was decided that careful precautions were sufficient. She has never been hurt; the worst that happens to her is that she gets dirty from the soot and mud—the troopers have to wipe her off or hose her down when she comes home. Mattie is a healthy, cheerful, lovable dog.

After a fire in which arson is suspected, Mattie searches the wreckage for the scent of an accelerant.   CONNECTICUT STATE POLICE CANINE UNIT

In a practice exercise, Mattie quickly finds the can on the daisy wheel that has the drop of a chemical in it.

Training Exercise for Mattie

On the training field of the Connecticut State Police Canine Unit there's an odd-looking contraption called a daisy wheel. It consists of two long, wooden planks set one across the other to form an **X** and secured on a pivot at the middle, so that the planks can spin like a wheel. At the ends of each plank, a large tin can is fastened.

Trooper Jim Butterworth shows off Mattie's skill.

A mere speck of a flammable liquid is put in the bottom of one can; it is a drop so small that no human nose can detect it. Now the wheel is spun. When it stops, nobody knows which can contains the chemical.

Mattie quickly checks out the cans. When she comes to the one that has the chemical in it and catches the scent, she sits down. Like Jackpot of the Department of Agriculture's Beagle Brigade, Mattie has been trained to give a passive response.

"Show me, Mattie!" Jim urges her. "Show me!"

Mattie makes a little darting gesture with her head, clearly indicating the can with her nose, and looks up at Jim.

She quickly and delicately points out the can again, and looks at her handler as if to say, "There it is, so where's my treat?"

"Good girl!" says Jim, giving her a treat.

Now, behind Mattie's back, a speck of accelerant is dropped on the grass between the arms of the daisy wheel. But Mattie isn't fooled—she finds it and receives her treat.

"After Mattie became expert on the daisy wheel, we began taking her to actual fire scenes that were not under investigation," explains Jim. "One of us would put a drop of gasoline on some spot in the wreckage and let her find it. That way she could transfer what she had learned on the wheel to the sort of place where she'd be using it."

If other fire investigation authorities around the country become convinced of Mattie's expertise, she may be the prototype—the first of a kind that is used as a model for others to follow.

The Canine Unit

Out on the field of the Connecticut State Police Canine Unit training center, state troopers are putting their dogs through their paces.

These are all people who volunteered to become canine handlers and were carefully screened before being admitted to the training course. They must not only learn how to control their highly sensitive and intelligent dogs but must also earn the animals' loyalty and trust.

Both male and female troopers or police officers can apply, provided they have good records and can properly house and care for a dog. Like the dogs of the New York City Police and of many police departments nationwide, the Connecticut troopers' dogs live at home with them. Mattie,

Troopers of the Connecticut State Police Canine Unit train with their dogs.

who works with three handlers, has three homes; she spends a week at each in turn.

Most of the dogs are German shepherds, though there are also some black Labrador retrievers and bloodhounds among them. But they have several things in common: large size (Doug Lancelot's seven-year-old German shepherd, Cato, weighs 105 pounds!), good health, and intelligence. While they must have an even temperament, they must be capable of aggression. A major reason that some dogs flunk out is that they cannot be roused to aggression—they are too much like good-natured pets. A trooper must be able to count on his dog to attack on command in a situation that calls for it. The dogs are not trained to inflict serious harm or to kill; they will bite and hold a person by the arm or leg.

All the dogs have been privately donated. About one-third of the German shepherds have been given to the canine unit by the Fidelco Guide Dog Foundation, an organization in Bloomfield, Connecticut, that breeds and trains superior dogs for the blind. Whenever Fidelco has a surplus of male dogs, or dogs with assertive temperaments that would make them unsuitable as guide dogs, they donate them to the state police. The troopers know that even though a dog has been rejected by an experienced Fidelco trainer because it might not be right for a blind person, that same dog could make an excellent state police dog—healthy, intelligent, alert, and brave, but requiring strong handling.

This day, the dogs are working first on obedience, learning both voice commands and hand signals. They pay attention and seem to be doing their best, even enjoying their lesson. Then they move to the obstacle course. Like other police dogs and search-and-rescue dogs, they must keep fit and be unafraid to climb ladders and leap over barriers. Some of these big dogs have trouble scrambling up the ladders and need a boost from their handlers, but eventually they'll master all the obstacles.

The training of a dog-and-handler team takes thirteen weeks. Dogs that pass are certified for obedience, tracking and trailing, evidence retrieval, building search, and crowd control. They must train one day a month to keep up their certification.

"In cases where we have to control crowds, such as at strikes or demonstrations, often just the appearance of our dogs walking on leashes is enough to keep things orderly," states Doug. "In fact, a dog may not even have to appear— there have been instances when some kind of disturbance like a street fight was going on, and we've driven up in our police car and let the dog bark into the loudspeaker. That can quiet things down real fast!"

The Connecticut State Police dogs are called upon almost daily throughout the state to hunt for missing persons. "A good dog will use all three search methods—tracking, trailing, and air scenting," Doug says. "This is important, because if

During a workout, a big dog gets a boost on the ladder.

I'm hunting a criminal, I want a dog that will be able to pick up his scent on the air as well as on the ground. Otherwise, if the dog was only following tracks, the guy could double back and ambush me from behind before the dog knew he was there. Also, lost children don't walk in a straight line— you'd waste valuable time if the dog relied on trailing alone.

"One of our dogs discovered a homicide victim recently by air scenting," Doug continues. "He found the body buried in four feet of ground under a concrete slab. People don't realize that scent percolates up through the ground, and while we can't detect it, a dog's amazing nose will. And here's a grisly detail for you—somebody's pet dog came home recently dragging the remains of a human head. We have dog teams out now searching for the body.

"But for an upbeat story, Ziegen, one of our Fidelco dogs, was called to search for a man in a snowstorm. The man's car had gotten stuck in the snow and he had gotten out and tried to walk for help, but collapsed, unconscious. The temperature was only ten degrees, and he surely would have frozen to death if Ziegen hadn't found him. The searchers got him to a hospital and he lived. Ziegen got a medal."

Specialized Training

In addition to basic training, some of the dogs take postgraduate work in specialties such as drug or explosives detection. Jim Butterworth's dog, Rajah, like the United States Customs dogs, is trained to detect drugs. Cato, Doug's enormous German shepherd, who is also a Fidelco dog, took an additional ten weeks of training to become a specialist in explosives detection.

"Cato may be called out when there's a bomb threat at an airport, school, office building, store, or wherever," explains Doug. "Or when a visiting VIP comes to make a speech or accept an award, Cato will sweep the auditorium or banquet hall first. This sort of thing has become increasingly important in many cities today where there's a possibility of terrorism."

Cato will be called on the case when there's a bomb threat, or even the possibility of one. His fine nose can detect the most commonly used explosives.

Cato can detect the most commonly used explosives: dynamite, TNT, black powder, smokeless powder, and plastic. His training was similar to that of many of the other dogs who do scent detection work—letting the dog smell an object, hiding the object, encouraging the dog to search for it, and rewarding him when he finds it.

Cato was taught passive response; obviously, when a dog finds an explosive device, it is crucial that he not disturb it. If he pounced on it or nudged it, he could blow up himself, his handler, and everybody and everything else! Like Mattie, Cato alerts by sitting. His reward is a game of ball with Doug.

Some of the United States Customs drug detector dogs also detect explosives. In one training exercise, a recently fired

Trooper Doug Lancelot hid an explosive under the hood of this car. Cato finds it, but never tries to disturb it. Instead, he signals to Doug by sitting alertly.

pistol was hidden in a cargo building at Kennedy Airport, and a handler, Canine Enforcement Officer Barbara Wilson, brought her six-year-old yellow Labrador, Shane, to search for it.

Barbara led Shane up and down between the stacked crates. When the dog suddenly sat down, she knew he had caught the scent of the gunpowder from the pistol. "Show me, Shane!" urged Barbara. "Show me!"

Shane stood up, stepped close to the crate where the gun was hidden, made a very quick point with his nose in its direction, and returned to a sit. "It's in here," he seemed to say, repeating the pointing gesture with his head. His reward was a game with his rolled-up towel.

"Not long ago, Shane alerted to a crate of firecrackers from China," his handler says.

Connecticut State Trooper Doug Lancelot is enthusiastic about the many possibilities for using a dog's highly sensitive scenting ability. "We can train a dog to smell out anything," he says. "People, evidence, drugs, explosives, other animals, agricultural products, hazardous wastes—the list is endless. Dogs are superior to machines in so many types of detection.

"We've only begun to discover all the things dogs can learn to do."

Additional Reading

More Than a Friend: Dogs with a Purpose. By Mary-Ellen Siegel and Hermine M. Koplin. Photographs by Stephanie Bee Koplin. New York: Walker, 1985. Stories of dogs trained to serve in police patrol, detect drugs and explosives, and guide blind, deaf, and otherwise handicapped people.

Jackpot of the Beagle Brigade. By Sam and Beryl Epstein. Photographs by George Ancona. New York: Macmillan, 1987. Photo essay about the Department of Agriculture's most famous detector dog and his handler, Hal Fingerman.

Law Enforcement Dogs. By Phyllis Raybin Emert. Mankato, Minnesota: Crestwood House, 1985. Descriptions of the training and work of police patrol dogs, and narcotics and explosives detector dogs.

Search and Rescue Dogs. By Phyllis Raybin Emert. Mankato, Minnesota: Crestwood House, 1985. Descriptions of the training and work of search-and-rescue dogs and Department of Agriculture beagles.

Friend to Friend: Dogs That Help Mankind. By Charlotte Schwartz. New York: Howell, 1984. Overview of working dogs, including therapy dogs, detector dogs, search-and-rescue dogs.

Search Dog Training. By Sandy Bryson. The Boxwood Press (183 Ocean View Boulevard, Pacific Grove, CA 93950), 1984. Written for professionals by a professional, but of interest to any dog lover, about the training of search-and-rescue dogs and detector dogs.

Directory of Search-and-Rescue Dog Organizations

Following is a list of search-and-rescue dog organizations that can be contacted for information. It is reprinted here courtesy of Marian Hardy, a member of DOGS-East and a board member of the National Association for Search and Rescue.

Alaska

Alaska Search and Rescue Dogs, Bill Tai, Suite 655, 200 West 34 Avenue, Anchorage, AK 99503. (907) 273-DOGS

P.A.W.S., Sally Berry, P.O. Box 81590, Fairbanks, AK 99708. (907) 455-6893

SEADOGS, Bruce Bowler, P.O. Box 244, Juneau, AK 99802. (907) 465-2985

Search Dogs Valdez, Box 2552, Valdez, AK 99686.

Arizona

Southern Arizona Rescue Association, Jerri Blackman, P.O. Box 66332, Tucson, AZ 85725. (602) 792-0701

California

Butte County SAR, Jim McCurry, Route 4, Box 525-Q, Chico, CA 95926. (916) 895-1616

California Rescue Dog Association, Shirley Hammond, 1062 Metro Circle, Palo Alto, CA 94303. (415) 856-9669

115

California-Swiss Search Dog Association, Willie Grundherr, 1203 Granite Creek Road, Santa Cruz, CA 95065. (408) 425-7661

Contra Costa County Bloodhounds, Judy Robb, 421 La Vista Road, Walnut Creek, CA 94598. (415) 939-9279

Los Angeles Search Dog Association, Jerry Newcomb, 3224 Mountain Curve, Altadena, CA 91001. (818) 798-7616

Monterey Bay Search Dogs, Carl Parsons, P.O. Box 1013, Aptos, CA 95001.

Sierra Madre Search and Rescue Team, Arnold Gaffrey, 9527 Wedgewood, Temple City, CA 91780. (818) 286-8053

WOOF Search Dogs, Marin County Sheriff's Department, Civic Center, San Rafael, CA 94903. (415) 499-7243

Canada

Alberta Bloodhound SAR, Rod Gow, Box 274, Bragg Creek, Alberta, Canada TOL-OKO. (403) 949-2054

Canadian Search and Rescue Dogs (CANSARD), Bill Grimmer, P.O. Box 126, Scoudouc, NB, Canada EOA-INO. (506) 532-4988

Colorado

Front Range Rescue Dogs, Ann Wichmann, 417 Sherman, Longmont, CO 80501. (303) 776-3957

Larimer County Search and Rescue, Fran Lieser, 4216 Glade Road, Loveland, CO 80537. (303) 667-9931

Montezuma County K-9 SAR Team, Lori Watkins, 337 North Ash, Cortez, CO 81321. (303) 565-6141

Search and Rescue Dogs of Colorado (SARDOC), Fran Lieser, same as Larimer County SAR, above.

Georgia

Georgia K-9 Rescue Association, Sandra Crain, P.O. Box 12, Cusseta, GA 31805. (404) 989-3464

Idaho

Mountain West Rescue Dogs, Michael Anderson, 509 Spokane Street, Coeur D'Alene, ID 83814. (208) 664-5691

Illinois

Illini Search and Rescue Service, Marj Kantak, 1106 South Fern Drive, Mount Prospect, IL 60056. (312) 956-0462

Illinois/Wisconsin SAR Dogs, Patti Gibson, P.O. Box 894, Woodstock, IL 60098. (815) 459-6523

Kansas

Lenexa Canine Unit, Paul Lee, 12500 West 87th Street, Lenexa, KS 66205.

Maine

Maine Search and Rescue Dogs, Jennifer Applegate, 80 Ledgelawn Avenue, Bar Harbor, ME 04609. (207) 288-5113

Maryland / Virginia

DOGS-East, Marian Hardy, 4 Orchard Way North, Rockville, MD 20854. (301) 762-7217

Michigan

DOGS-North, Sally Santeford, Route 1, Box 332, Houghton, MI 49931. (906) 482-5135

Minnesota

Minnesota Search and Rescue Dog Association, John Shelton, 6840 Washington Street NE, Fridley, MN 55432. (612) 572-9358

Search Dogs, Inc., Mary Jane Dyer, 3310 Wren Lane, Eagan, MN 55121. (612) 452-4209

Mississippi

Desoto County Emergency Management Council, Al Coveney, 325 Star Landing Road, Nesbit, MS 38651. (601) 368-5965

Missouri

Mid-America Rescue Dog Association, Karen Brown, HCR 77, Box 17-1, Sunrise Beach, MO 65079. (314) 374-6388

Missouri Search and Rescue K-9, Irene Korotev, 8307 Winchester, Kansas City, MO 64138. (816) 356-9097

Odessa VFD Bloodhounds, Orville Day, 809 West Pleasant, Odessa, MO 64076. (816) 633-5396

Montana

Absaroka Search Dogs, Vikki F. Bowman, Box 22081, Billings, MT 59104. (406) 245-7335

Black Paws Search, Rescue, and Avalanche Dogs, Susie Richter, P.O. Box 684, Bigfork, MT 59911. (406) 837-5547

Search Dogs North, Sandra West, P.O. Box 5254, Missoula, MT 59806. (406) 721-2153

New Hampshire

New England K-9 Search and Rescue, Annabella Fowler, RFD 2, Box 143, Antrim, NH 03440. (603) 588-2413

New Jersey

Palisades Search and Rescue Dog Association, Cindy Geaneas, 225 Vreeland Avenue, Boonton, NJ 07005. (201) 334-6204

Ramapo Rescue Dog Association, Emil J. Pelcak, 247 Airmount Avenue, Ramsey, NJ 07446. (201) 327-0961

West Jersey Canine Search and Rescue, Millie Curtis, P.O. Box 384, Bloomsbury, NJ 08804. (201) 479-4214

New Mexico

Albuquerque Rescue Dog Association, Diana Pappan, 1037 Stuart NW, Albuquerque, NM 87114. (505) 898-4028

Cibola Search and Rescue, Bruce Berry, 10723 Edith NE, Albuquerque, NM 87113. (505) 897-3652

Four Corners SAR, Percy Langley, P.O. Box 1921, Farmington, NM 87499.

New Mexico Rescue Dogs, Bob Foster, 80 Raven Road, Tijeras, NM 87059. (505) 281-3975

New York

Adirondack Rescue Dog Association, Marilyn Green, 5028 Juniper Lane, Schenectady, NY 12303. (518) 356-2431

American Rescue Dog Association, Penny Sullivan, P.O. Box 151, Chester, NY 10918. (914) 469-4173

Rensselaer County Search and Rescue Team, David Onderdonk, Onderdonk Avenue, Rensselaer, NY 12144. (518) 477-9267
Wilderness Search and Rescue Team of NY State, Fred DeHart, 831 Grange Road, Homer, NY 13077.

North Carolina
Blue Ridge Search and Rescue Dogs, Brenda Davis, 225 Steward Road, Waynesville, NC 28786.
North Carolina Search and Rescue Association, Denver Holder, P.O. Box 956, Clyde, NC 28721. (704) 648-3851

Ohio
Athens Search, Track and Rescue Association, John Tobin, 74 East State Street, Athens, OH 45701. (614) 592-4630

Oklahoma
SAR Dogs of Oklahoma, Mike Nozer, 5015 East 33 Street, Tulsa, OK 74135. (918) 749-1546
Western Ozark Bloodhound Team, Elsa Gann, Route 2, Box 162, Collinsville, OK 74021.

Oregon
Oregon DOGS, 15842 South Ames, Oregon City, OR 97045.

Pennsylvania
Department of Environmental Resources SAR Unit, Ken Boyles, RD 3, P.O. Box 2272, Newville, PA 17241. (717) 776-7949
Greensburg Fire Department Bloodhound Team, Edward Hutchinson, 318 Alexander Avenue, Greensburg, PA 15601. (412) 834-7365
Northeast Search and Rescue, Bruce Barton, P.O. Box 162, Stroudsburg, PA 18360. (717) 424-1883
Rescue 40, Al and Pat Yessel, RD 1, Lancaster Road, Fombell, PA 16123. (412) 752-1402

Tennessee
Chattanooga STARS, Jim Poplin, P.O. Box 1008, Chattanooga, TN 37401. (404) 861-1730

Morristown Emergency and Rescue Squad, Jackye Byrd, 420 North Jackson Street, Morristown, TN 37814. (615) 581-4469

Texas

C.E.S.A.R., Cynthia Giles, 1701 Vinewood, Fort Worth, TX 76112. (817) 654-1842

North Texas Volunteer Mantrailers, Teri Anglim, 3805 Misty Meadow, Fort Worth, TX 76133. (817) 294-8740

Starr County Sheriff K-9 Unit, Eugenio Falcon, Jr., Starr County Courthouse, Rio Grande City, TX 78582.

Texas Association of EMTs—Dog Unit, Ronald Perry, 3010 Sierra Drive, San Angelo, TX 76904. (915) 944-2139

Volunteer SAR K-9 Unit, David Elbers, Route 7, Box 524E, Mission, TX 78572.

Utah

Rocky Mountain Rescue Dogs, Dick Epley, 745 East 5400 South, Ogden, UT 84405. (801) 479-4265

Vermont

Vermont SAR Dog Service, Mary Anne Gummere, P.O. Box 244, Glover, VT 05839. (802) 525-4128

Virginia

Blue and Gray Search and Rescue Dogs, Vickie Michael, Route 3, Box 272-1, Dayton, VA 22821. (703) 879-9684

Colonial Heights SAR Unit, Willie Jenkins, 903 Kensington Avenue, Colonial Heights, VA 23834. (804) 520-2056

Sussex County Sheriff's Office, Philip Andrews, Route 2, Box 172-A, Disputanta, VA 23842. (804) 834-3528

Tidewater Trail Search and Rescue Team, John Branyon, 111 Creek Circle, Seaford, VA 23696. (804) 898-7118

Washington

Cascade Dogs, Kathy and Rick Fifer, 129 Wiatrak Road, Morton, WA 98356. (206) 496-5184

German Shepherd Search Dogs of Washington State, P.O. Box 466, Kirkland, WA 98083. (206) 876-8939

Justice Search Dogs (Windy Valley Mantrailers), Jan Tweedie, 12309 SE 164th, Renton, WA 98058. (206) 255-6852
Northwest Bloodhounds SAR, Lena Reed, 10705 Woodland Avenue, Puyallup, WA 98373. (206) 845-8039
Sandpoint Cadet Squadron Bloodhound Team, Tim Vik, 7309 Sandpoint Way NE, #838, Seattle, WA 98115. (206) 526-0332
West Coast Search Dogs of Washington, Terre Reeson, 512 West Fifth Street, Hoquiam, WA 98550. (206) 533-2790

Wisconsin

Headwaters Search and Rescue Dog Association, Burt Mattson, 4710 Grosser Lane, Phelps, WI 54554. (715) 545-2671
RescuMed Dog Association, Lori Wick, 1304 West Terminal Road, Grafton, WI 53024. (414) 375-0456
Wilderness SAR, Toni Woodie, Route 1, Box 25-A, Butternut, WI 54514. (715) 769-3589

Wyoming

Jackson Hole Search Dogs, Linda Waggoner, 1949 Sheridan Avenue, Cody, WY 82414.

Index

About the Author

Patricia Curtis is the author of many books and magazine articles about animals. Of *Dogs on the Case* she says, "My book is a tribute to these highly trained search dogs and to the skilled people who work with them. I hope readers will enjoy learning about these wonderful dogs and the important jobs they do."

Ms. Curtis is the mother of two grown children and has one young grandson. She lives in New York City with her dog and four cats.

About the Photographer

David Cupp is a writer-photographer whose articles and pictures have appeared frequently in *National Geographic Magazine*. He and Patricia Curtis also collaborated on *All Wild Creatures Welcome, The Animal Shelter,* and *Cindy, A Hearing Ear Dog*. He is Director of Photography at the Press-Enterprise in Riverside, California, where he lives with his wife and three children.